MORTIMER'S CROSS

A CHARLOTTE ZOLOTOW BOOK

JOAN AIKEN

MORTIMER'S CROSS

containing

The Mystery of Mr. Jones's Disappearing Taxi
Mortimer's Cross
Mortimer's Portrait on Glass

pictures by Quentin Blake

1 8  1 7

———————— HARPER & ROW, PUBLISHERS ————————

Cambridge, Philadelphia, San Francisco, London, Mexico City, São Paulo, Sydney

———————— NEW YORK ————————

MORTIMER'S CROSS
This collection was first published in 1983 by the British Broadcasting
Corporation, London. *The Mystery of Mr. Jones's Disappearing Taxi* and
Mortimer's Portrait on Glass were first published by BBC/Knight in 1982.

Library of Congress Cataloging in Publication Data
Aiken, Joan, 1924–
  Mortimer's cross.

  "A Charlotte Zolotow book."
  Sequel to: Arabel and Mortimer.
  Summary: Three further adventures of Arabel and her
pet raven, Mortimer, include "The Mystery of Mr. Jones's
Disappearing Taxi," "Mortimer's Cross," and "Mortimer's
Portrait on Glass."
  [1. Ravens—Fiction. 2. Humorous stories] I. Blake,
Quentin, ill. II. Title.
PZ7.A2695Mp 1984   [Fic]   83-49475
ISBN 0-06-020032-4
ISBN 0-06-020033-2 (lib. bdg.)

1 2 3 4 5 6 7 8 9 10
First American Edition

CONTENTS

THE MYSTERY OF MR. JONES'S DISAPPEARING TAXI

1

Things were a bit gloomy in the Jones household. Firstly, between Guy Fawkes Day and Christmas there had been only two days when it hadn't rained. This made everybody bad tempered.

Arabel Jones couldn't practice on her new skateboard.

Mortimer the raven couldn't chase the next-door cat.

Mrs. Jones couldn't stroll about the shopping precinct with her sister Brenda.

Mr. Jones was the only person who didn't mind the wet weather: People ride in taxis much more when it is wet, and as he was a taxi driver the rain brought him plenty of customers. But he had a grievance of his own: the gas men were digging a trench all the way along Rainwater Crescent, where the Joneses lived (and being very slow about it, because their trench kept filling up with rain and having to be pumped out). All the time they were digging the trench, which seemed to have gone on for weeks and weeks, Mr. Jones had not been able to park his taxi outside his own front door, but had, instead, to leave it in the parking lot at the end of the street. And the result of leaving it in the parking lot had been very strange.

"Blest if I know why it is," grumbled Mr. Jones one

morning at breakfast, "but the old bus seems to use a deal more fuel than she done before."

"Oh, dear, Ben, perhaps you need a new taxi," said Mrs. Jones, putting on her coat to go and be a temporary receptionist at a hairdressers' salon for two hours.

"Rubbish, Martha, I've only had this cab five years!" said Mr. Jones. "A good taxi can last twenty years, properly looked after, that is."

"P'raps it doesn't *like* being left in the parking lot," suggested Arabel.

Just then Chris Cross came to take Arabel to the public library. Arabel had lately become very fond of reading, and as Chris spent a lot of time at the library because he was studying for his college entrance exams, he had agreed to take Arabel along whenever he went. This suited Mrs. Jones, as when Arabel was at the library she could do part-time work for an agency that supplied offices with temporary help. The only problem about this arrangement was Mortimer, Arabel's raven. Mrs. Jones flatly refused to leave him alone in the house when she went out, because of the unheard-of damage he was likely to cause if not kept under observation. Mortimer was very fond of eating wire, and had once wrecked the electrical system by chewing up every inch of the wire in the house when Mrs. Jones ran out to the shop for five minutes for a cauliflower, taking Arabel with her; while another time he got stuck inside the clothes dryer, causing it to hop all over the floor, overturn the kitchen table, and turn twenty pots of marmalade that Mrs. Jones had just made into a shambles of broken glass and squish.

Consequently Mrs. Jones insisted that Mortimer must accompany Chris and Arabel on their visits to the library. Arabel was always happy to have Mortimer with her, but Miss Acaster, the head librarian, gave a shudder whenever she saw Mortimer come through the entrance.

"Ready, Arabel?" said Chris Cross. "Got the books you're taking back? You don't need your raincoat today; the forecast said 'Fine and Dry.' Just fancy!"

"Then I'll take my skateboard," said Arabel. She picked it up, as well as *Splendors of the Heavens*, *Freud Explained to the Children*, and *The Bad Child's Book of Beasts*.

"Mind—you're not to go in the road with that skateboard, Arabel dearie," said Mrs. Jones.

"No. I'll go under Rumbury Tower Heights," said Arabel.

"And mind you're home sharp at one," said Mrs. Jones.

"Yes, Ma," said Arabel, putting on her duffel coat, which was convenient for Mortimer because he could sit in the hood; and did.

"Mr. Jones," said Chris, "isn't the license plate of your taxi JON 333N?"

"Yes, it is," said Mr. Jones. "Why?"

"Were you driving about at five this morning?"

"No, I most certainly was *not*," said Mr. Jones. "Up before seven, dead before eleven. Why?"

"Well, I was up at five because I'm doing temporary post work," said Chris, "and I saw your taxi being driven across Rumbury Marsh."

"You did *what*?" said Mr. Jones, his eyes popping.

"Saw your taxi! I ought to know it anyway," said Chris, "I've cleaned it often enough. I recognized the dent in the bumper, let alone the license number."

"Then some so-and-so's pinching it at night and using it," said Mr. Jones, "and *that's* why it's been so heavy on the gas lately! Just wait till I get my hands on the perisher! I'll make him sorry he ever learned to drive! I'll lay for him at the parking lot this very night."

"I'll come too," said Chris, "with my motorbike. Then we can follow him and see where he goes."

"Oh yes! I'll come too!" cried Arabel. "And we could put Mortimer inside the taxi—hidden in the glove compartment—then he could pop out presently and give the thief a fright. He'd like that, wouldn't you, Mortimer?"

"KAAARK!" said Mortimer, his eyes shining.

"Well, we'll see, we'll see, we'll see about that," said Mr. Jones, not quite certain as to that part of the plan.

Mrs. Jones had gone out by this time, or she would undoubtedly have disapproved, very strongly indeed.

Arabel and Chris went off to the library with Mortimer sitting in the hood of Arabel's duffel coat.

Rumbury Public Library was a handsome new building, built on the edge of Rumbury Marshes and the long road that was called Rumbury Waste. The library was round, like a gasometer, but had many more windows, and there were all sorts of modern gadgets inside. For instance, there was a copier. You put 5 pence in a slot, and then it would copy any letter or picture that you laid under a rubber flap on top. Mortimer used to try to get a copy of himself (whenever Arabel had 5 pence to spare)—but he could never lie flat enough under the flap to make the copier work properly. Still, he loved the bright light and the humming noise it made; and he used to annoy people a good deal, when they were trying to make copies of things, by suddenly rushing up from behind them and diving headfirst under the flap just as the light was shining.

Then there was a huge electric index of all the books in the library: You pressed a knob and the names of the books came up on a screen, and you turned another knob which made all the titles roll upward, right through the alphabet. Mortimer loved turning the second knob very fast, and whizzing the books through from *Aardvarks at Home* to *Zebra Training for Beginners*. But Miss Acaster was not at all keen on Mortimer doing this.

The various other people who used the library were never very pleased, either, when they saw Mortimer come in. His visits nearly always seemed to end in some kind of disturbance; he liked to climb on the trolley where the returned books were stacked, and shove it along with his wings at a fearful speed; or he flew up to the gallery where the reference books were kept, and dropped dictionaries over the rail onto people's heads; or he just climbed around from one shelf to another, muttering loudly to himself, and sometimes shouting "Nevermore!" in a very loud and distracting way.

Mortimer was not a restful bird.

There was one little man, however, who always noticed Arabel and Mortimer when they came into the library; his name was Mr. Beeline. We shall return to him later.

On this particular morning Miss Acaster walked over to Arabel very fast, as soon as she came in. "We are always happy to see *you*, my dear," Miss Acaster said firmly, "but your bird must stay outside."

"Oh, but please, he *always* comes in," said Arabel. "I don't think he'd be happy if he was left outside! And when he's unhappy he gets cross, and when he's cross he does things that are inconvenient."

"He is *just* as inconvenient *inside*," said Miss Acaster. "I'm afraid he must stay out. A new regulation has been passed by the library committee, and it is to be strictly enforced."

She pointed to a card that said:

NO RAVENS IN THE LIBRARY.

BY ORDER.

"Oh dear," said Arabel. "Well, in that case, Mortimer, I'm afraid you'll have to stay out on the terrace. I'll be as quick as I can."

Strangely enough, Mortimer did not seem too upset at being made to wait outside. He sat on the open stone terrace and looked across Rumbury Marshes at a huge high-rise building that had been put up there a couple of years before. It was called Rumbury Tower Heights. Mortimer seemed very interested in it.

When Arabel had chosen her books—*Mathematics for Moppets, Advanced Skateboarding,* and *Flower Fairies of the Autumn*—she came to the counter to have them stamped.

She heard two of the librarians talking together.

"It wouldn't surprise *me* if it was that raven that was responsible for all the books that have been stolen from the library in the last six months," said Mr. Trigg, the under-librarian. "Over a thousand books! It's scandalous!"

Arabel was indignant. "Mortimer has never stolen a single book!" she said. "He does like to *eat* books, I know, but I don't let him. He has never eaten a single library book."

"Well, I'm glad to hear it," said Mr. Trigg, but he did not sound as if he believed Arabel.

"I'll be outside," Arabel whispered to Chris, who was reading at a table. He nodded and she went out. On the terrace, Mortimer was still gazing at Rumbury Tower Heights.

"Shall we go over there and skate, Mortimer?" said Arabel.

There was a bit of grassy, weedy waste ground between the library and the tower building. It was always damp, because it was really Rumbury Marsh. Nobody wanted to build anything on it, because it flooded every winter, sooner or later—and sometimes in the summer too.

Arabel walked over the soggy grass (luckily she was

wearing rubber boots) to the tower building. It was twenty stories high, and stood on twelve legs. Underneath, in among the legs, was a wide stretch of concrete pavement, just right for skateboards. In the middle of the pavement was a fountain. This was like a stone tank, about the length of two buses standing end to end. All along inside the tank, jets of water shot up. They were quite high— in fact they shot as high as the ceiling, which was the underside of the tower block. Arabel was very fond of the fountain. She stood looking at it for a long time. So did Mortimer. First one jet would slowly let itself down until it was almost gone. Then it would shoot up again, higher and higher, till it hit the ceiling. Then the next one would do the same thing.

"Wouldn't it be lovely to sit on one of those jets, Mortimer," Arabel said, as she always did.

"Kaaaark," said Mortimer, as he always did.

Then Arabel carefully put down the plastic bag containing her library books. She put her skateboard on the ground, got onto it, pushed herself off with one foot, and went gliding away. She wove a complicated course in between the twelve thick pillars that held the tower block above her, winding in and out, going round and round the fountain. Mortimer rode happily in the hood of her duffel coat, singing a one-word, one-note song to himself, over and over. It went: "Nevermore. Nevermore. Never, never, never, never, never, nevermore."

They were the only people there.

Nobody lived in Rumbury Tower Heights, or worked

there. A firm had built the block three years before, and advertised it for office and business premises, but they had asked such enormous rents that no one wanted to use the building, and it stood empty.

Six months ago there had been an indignant headline in the *Rumbury Gazette*:

RUMBURY TOWER STILL STANDS EMPTY.
WHY DOES NOT THE COUNCIL STEP IN?

Actually the ones who had stepped in were a colony of bats, who had discovered it and nested there; they liked it because most of the windows were shuttered, which made a comfortable darkness for them. Professor Pook, a very learned natural historian, had been to look at the bats, and had got very excited about them because they were a rare and large species, not usually found in England. He had the whole building declared a Bat

Sanctuary. Now nobody was supposed to go into it at all, for fear of disturbing the bats, except a building inspector, who looked in once a month to make sure the place was safe and not likely to fall down. And *he* stayed no longer than he absolutely had to.

"Proper spooky it is, I'm glad to get out of there, I can tell you," he said. "Firstly there's no power, no lights, no heat, no elevator, you has to walk up all them stairs and it's as cold and dark as the inside of a deep-freeze. And, second, there's all them blinkin' bats hanging up-side down looking right nasty—some of them have got a wingspread of over five foot, I give you my word."

Indeed Professor Pook said this was quite possible, as they were Kalong bats from the East Indies; no doubt they had arrived in Rumbury Dock on some fruit boat.

Mortimer loved scooting around in Arabel's hood un-derneath the tower block, as he had very sharp ears, and he could hear the bats squeaking and snoring up above. He often planned to visit the bats; but he had not yet found out how to get into Rumbury Tower Heights. He was still thinking about this project.

Other people were also interested in visiting Rum-bury Tower Heights.

"There comes Chris," Arabel said presently. "Time to go home, Mortimer."

"Kaaark," said Mortimer, staring thoughtfully up at the tops of the fountain jets, where they hit the roof.

He was very silent all the way home in Arabel's hood.

2

That evening, when Mr. Jones came in, he said, "I've decided to do what young Chris said."

"What's that, Ben?" Mrs. Jones asked. However, just at that moment, the part-time job agency phoned to ask if Mrs. Jones could go around to the offices of Rumbury Pirate Radio for a couple of hours, as their receptionist had gone home with a nosebleed.

Mrs. Jones put on her coat and went off, reminding Arabel and her father that Arabel's bedtime was eight-thirty sharp.

Mr. Jones glanced out of the window. It was as dark outside as the inside of a rubber boot, but it was not raining, nor particularly cold; he said, "Come on, Arabel; I'm going down to the parking lot to look out for that tea-leaf who's been pinching my taxi."

"Oh yes!" said Arabel with enthusiasm, and she ran to put on her duffel coat again, and tucked Mortimer into the hood. They stopped at the Cross house (which was next door) and invited Chris to come along too, which he did, scooting on his motorbike beside them.

When they got to the parking lot they could see that Mr. Jones's taxi was in its usual spot, right at this end, near the turnstile, which was left open at night.

"So the thief hasn't been yet," said Chris.

"Do let's put Mortimer inside," said Arabel. "Then he can give the thief a terrible fright, can't you, Mortimer."

"Kaark," said Mortimer.

"But," objected Mr. Jones, "suppose he gives him such a fright that the guy runs my taxi into a lamp post and dents it?"

However, in the end Mr. Jones was persuaded to allow Mortimer to get into the taxi and hide in the glove compartment; firstly because, he said, "That bird might as well make himself useful somehow; dear knows he eats enough"; and secondly because after they had waited half an hour or so, hiding behind the hedge, Mortimer began to be a bit of a nuisance, grumbling and shouting "Nevermore," and Mr. Jones was afraid he might give away the ambush. So Mortimer was put into the glove compartment and told to keep quiet.

Inside the glove compartment, Mortimer promptly fell asleep.

The watchers did not have long to wait (luckily, for the clock on Rumbury Town Hall was visible from where they were hiding and Arabel could see that it said 8:45). A small dark figure slipped along between the lines of cars, unlocked the door of Mr. Jones's taxi ("Cor!" whispered Mr. Jones. "The son-of-a-gun must have had a duplicate key made!"), started up the motor, and drove away rapidly, along Canal Road.

Immediately, Chris Cross threw a leg over his motorbike; Mr. Jones, holding Arabel, got on the pillion behind him; and Chris started up his engine. None too soon; for the taxi lights were almost out of sight.

Chris was after it in a flash; and Mr. Jones had plenty of time to regret his decision to allow Arabel to come with them. "Martha will never forgive me for this," he groaned to himself, as the motorbike wound swiftly in and out of traffic, shot over pedestrian crossings and traffic lights, needled its way through tiny gaps, whizzed across roundabouts, zipped between level-crossing gates,

and bounded over bridges. The thief seemed to be joy-riding all over Rumbury Town.

Arabel was having the time of her life. "I'm sorry Mortimer's missing this," she thought. "It's even better than skateboarding. When I'm bigger, I'll get a motor-bike just like Chris's."

"Have we lost the perisher?" yelled Mr. Jones to Chris.

"I think he went this way," Chris yelled back over his shoulder.

He was now going in the direction of Rumbury Public Library. However, when they reached it, there was no taxi to be seen.

"Hey, what's that, then?" said Chris.

There was a light crossing the marsh. Chris acceler-ated, and zipped along the side of Rumbury Waste. Then he turned left.

"*Is* that him ahead?"

"Yeah, yeah," said Chris. "I think so."

"Is he driving natural-like?" said Mr. Jones, who couldn't see much because Chris's crash helmet was in the way.

"Seems to be," said Chris.

"Mortimer can't have let out his squawk yet," said Mr. Jones.

"Maybe he's biding his time," said Chris.

Some traffic lights ahead of them turned red; they had to wait. "Funny thing," said Chris, peering ahead. "Taxi seems to have stopped under the big tower— Rumbury Heights. What's he want to go there for?"

By the time Chris had come to a halt under the tower,

where Arabel had been skating earlier in the day, the taxi was parked quietly beside the fountain. But there was nobody inside it. No thief—and no Mortimer either. The glove compartment was empty.

"Oh, my goodness," Arabel said anxiously. "What can have happened to Mortimer?"

They all hunted about, among the pillars and behind the fountain. Nobody was there.

Arabel came back to the fountain and studied it thoughtfully. It was still fountaining, because it ran on solar heat, charging up enough energy in the daytime to keep it going all night. The jets of water looked very handsome, dyed bright yellow by the rays from the street lights along Rumbury Waste.

Mr. Jones and Chris were planning to lurk by the taxi until the thief reappeared. "Then we can catch him red-handed," said Mr. Jones. "But I suppose he may be a long time, if you saw him driving home at five in the morning," he added doubtfully, looking at Chris. "Arabel, dearie, maybe you'd better get into the cab. Then you can have a nap, see, and keep warm—and you'll be out o' the way, if there's any ruckus."

But there was no answer from Arabel, and, looking

around, Mr. Jones saw with alarm that she, too, had disappeared.

Meanwhile, over at the offices of Rumbury Pirate Radio, Mrs. Jones was having an interesting time. Rumbury Pirate Radio was run from a barge that was moored in the middle of Rumbury Canal, just where it ran into the River Thames; you reached the barge by going across a gangway, which made Mrs. Jones rather nervous. However, once inside, it seemed much like any other office; Mrs. Jones sat at a pink desk with a bunch of gladioli on it and a sign that said *Inquiries*. Her job was to answer the phone, and direct visitors where they should go. The agency had told Mrs. Jones that she was lucky to get this job, as she might see all kinds of celebrities, such as The Rocking Horses, or Foul Fred Fink, or Tuppenny Rice, or the Sewer Rats. But, as Mrs. Jones wasn't interested in pop music and knew nothing whatever about rock or punk, she might not have recognized Foul Fred Fink even if she had seen him.

In fact there were not many celebrities tonight. It was rather quiet. Mrs. Jones got a whole sleeve of a cardigan knitted for Arabel. Then the phone rang, and Mrs. Jones, picking up the receiver, said: "Rumbury Pirate Radio, can I help you?"

A low thick fierce voice hissed in her ear. It said: "Listen! We are the Hatmen! We have got Naughty Madge Owens, who is being kept in a secret hideaway where no one will ever think of searching. If a ransom of eight million pounds is not paid by next Thursday,

January the tenth, she will be weighted with twelve volumes of the *Complete Oxford Dictionary* and dropped into the Rumbury Canal."

"What?" shrieked Mrs. Jones.

"Eight million pounds for the return of Naughty Madge Owens! The money must be put into plastic garbage bags and left in the builders' rubbish skip that is standing outside the deserted asbestos factory near Rumbury Dock. Is that clear?"

"No!" gasped Mrs. Jones. But the caller had hung up.

Mrs. Jones immediately went into hysterics. She laughed, she cried, she wailed, she gurgled, she hiccuped, she screamed, she gibbered.

Quite soon, people began to come out of their offices, and ask her what was the matter.

"Oh!" wept Mrs. Jones. "They want eight million pounds put in plastic bags and taken to the asbestos factory. But how can we collect even *one* million pounds, let alone eight?"

"But *who* wants eight million? And why? And where is the asbestos factory? What is this all about, Mrs. Jones?"

"Those fiends have got our raven!"

"For heaven's sake, what fiends?"

"How should *I* know what fiends?" sobbed Mrs. Jones, rocking to and fro. "How should I know what horrible criminals have taken it into their wicked heads to go off with him, or why? But they've *got* him, that's for sure. Plain as I'm sitting here the disgusting wretch said, 'We have got Mortimer Jones!' And if they've got Mortimer, they *must* have Arabel too!"

Then she fainted dead away.

All the people at Rumbury Pirate Radio were very concerned for her, and they rushed about, burning feathers under her nose (fortunately there were plenty of these, because of the plentiful sea gulls always perching in the rigging and on the aerial and upsetting reception and dropping feathers on the deck); they also undid Mrs. Jones's collar and slapped her hands and gave her brandy and sal volatile to drink.

Of course it was pure bad luck for the kidnappers of Naughty Madge Owens that their phone message had been received by Mrs. Jones. She was very likely the only person in Rumbury Town (or indeed in London)—not counting Mortimer, that is—who had never heard of the famous pop singer. Naughty Madge Owens had been born plain Margaret in Walton-on-the-Naze and rechristened herself Naughty Madge when she became a singer. She had a huge and devoted fan club, several million strong, who would certainly have been happy to subscribe to the ransom. Eight million pounds would have been nothing to them. But because of Mrs. Jones's mistake, the news of Naughty Madge's abduction never got out.

When Mrs. Jones had recovered a little, the kind-hearted supervisor drove her home. But a lot of time was wasted because Mrs. Jones was gulping and choking so much that the supervisor thought she said she lived in Rayners Lane, not Rainwater Crescent.

When she finally did get home, Mrs. Jones was not surprised to find the house dark and empty. "Very likely the kidnappers have taken Ben, too," she tearfully said. "I'd better phone up my cousin Sam."

"Yes, you do that, dear," the supervisor kindly said. "And I'll stay till he comes."

Actually Mrs. Jones's cousin Sam Halliwell was a Detective Sergeant in Rumbury Police, and as soon as she had got him on the phone, Mrs. Jones screeched at him: "Sam, Sam, some horrible kidnappers have gone off with our Mortimer, and probably little Arabel and Ben

too, leastways nobody's at home, and they are going to drop Mortimer into Rumbury Canal weighted down with the *Oxford Dictionary*—in fact he's probably lying there already with his toes turned up, for we've not got the eight million nor likely to have it! So please, Sam, please, please drag the canal *at once*! Oh, I don't know what poor little Arabel will say, unless she's in the canal too, she'll just about break her heart."

Now of course Cousin Sam was not at all likely to have the Rumbury Canal dragged simply on the say-so of his cousin Martha, who had been known to get things wrong before, but in fact the Rumbury Police had received a tip-off that a gang called the Hatmen, who had started operating in the Rumbury area, might have sunk a consignment of stolen marshmallows in the canal, sealed in plastic containers. Accordingly, Sam said: "Well, Martha, we'll see what we can do. Where are you now?"

"I'm at home," wept Mrs. Jones.

"Well, you better stay right at home in case there's violence."

By now it was well into the middle of the night. Mrs. Jones hadn't the heart to go to bed, so she made herself a cup of tea and started knitting the second sleeve of Arabel's cardigan.

And, meanwhile, where *was* Naughty Madge Owens?

She had been snatched by the Hatmen. (The gang were called this because they all wore such extremely large hats that their faces were never seen.) They had recently come to England from the south of France, where they had read about the empty condition of Rumbury Tower Heights in the overseas edition of the *Daily Mail* (which had not, however, mentioned the bats). The Hatmen had got Naughty Madge imprisoned on the eighth floor of Rumbury Tower Heights, and they felt confident that they were going to make a lot of money from her. And they felt certain that Rumbury Tower Heights was going to make a very useful center of operations.

3

Meanwhile, what had happened to Arabel?

While Mr. Jones and Chris, underneath the tower block, were inspecting the empty taxi for marks of violence and not finding any, Arabel had noticed a small dark figure softly wheeling a cart into the dim distance. She quietly followed this figure, and getting closer to him, unobserved, noticed with interest that he was little Mr. Beeline from the public library! He was the person who always sat reading at a table in the corner, and had directed some particularly nasty looks at Mortimer; moreover his cart, the sort they have in supermarkets, was quite full of books. Arabel, very curious, followed Mr. Beeline and watched him get inside Rumbury Tower Heights by a very clever way.

There was a fire escape of openwork iron steps, going

zigzag right up the side of the building to the top. But it didn't quite reach the ground, in order to prevent burglars' making use of it. The bottom flight of steps was like a ladder on a spring; and as long as somebody was not actually *on* it, weighing it down, it swung up and stuck out sideways, eighteen feet up in the air, out of reach of anybody standing on the ground.

Mr. Beeline, however, had an umbrella with a telescopic stalk; he calmly pulled the handle out until it was long enough to reach up to the sideways ladder, and used the crook end to pull the steps down. Then he took the huge bundle of books from his cart (they were tied together with a rubber strap) and disappeared up the steps, staggering slightly under the weight of his

load. When he went inside, the steps sprang back to their original position.

"Well, I never!" thought Arabel. "So *he's* the thief who takes all the books from the library! And he uses Pa's taxi to bring them here! If I can find where he puts the books, I'll tell Miss Acaster, and then she'll be so pleased that perhaps she'll let Mortimer into the library again."

Occupied by this interesting plan, Arabel picked up Mr. Beeline's umbrella, which he had left lying by the empty cart, hooked down the steps in her turn, and followed Mr. Beeline. She had a strong suspicion, also, that Mortimer had somehow managed to get into the building, and she hoped that she might come across him.

And what *had* happened to Mortimer?

By the time Mr. Beeline had driven away the taxi, Mortimer, curled up in the glove compartment, was fast asleep. He woke up at the library, where Mr. Beeline halted to pick up the books he had previously hidden in a concrete litter bin. Mortimer was so interested when a large load of books was put in the back that he wasted no time shouting "Nevermore" to scare the driver, but just quietly ate the first three volumes of Edward Gibbon's *Decline and Fall of the Roman Empire*. These lasted him as far as Rumbury Tower Heights. Mr. Beeline never noticed Mortimer, and he quietly slipped from the taxi while Mr. Beeline was unloading his books, and walked over to the fountain.

For a long time, Mortimer had been wondering if it would be possible to sit on top of one of the fountain jets. The present time seemed a very good opportunity to try. While Mr. Beeline was wheeling cartloads of books back and forth to the fire escape, Mortimer clambered up the side of the stone tank that held the fountain, and waited until one of the end jets sank down as low as it would go. Then, as it started to rise again, Mortimer launched himself out with his wings—hop, flap—and landed exactly on top of the jet, which was so powerful that it did indeed begin to carry him up. Higher and higher went Mortimer.

"Kaaark!" he said joyfully. It was exactly like sitting on top of a rapidly growing palm tree. The fountain was rather cold underneath him, to be sure, but Mortimer did not mind that—his feathers were so thick and waterproof that the drops could not get through to his skin.

Up and up he went, nearly to the ceiling. And now, just above him, he could see a little trap-hole which was a ventilator in the floor of the bottom story of Rumbury Tower Heights. Mortimer grabbed the grating with his beak and claws, and then he managed to poke his way through between the bars.

So, at this time, both Arabel and Mortimer were in Rumbury Tower Heights.

Meanwhile, down below, Mr. Jones and Chris were becoming more and more anxious and alarmed, hunting far and wide among the pillars and on the grassy ground beyond, calling and calling: "Arabel! Mortimer! Where the devil are you? Where have you got to?"

"Oh, my goodness," said Mr. Jones, worried and guilty. "What Martha will say when she hears about this, I do

not know." Actually he did know, quite well. Or at least he had a pretty good idea.

Mr. Jones and Chris were so perturbed and distracted, wondering where Arabel and Mortimer had got to, that neither of them noticed three dark figures who arrived quietly and unobtrusively on bicycles, parked their bikes against one of the big pillars, pulled a lot of complicated equipment out of their saddlebags, and then proceeded to disappear *up* the pillar with a good deal of whispering, shushing, and giggling. Nor did Mr. Jones and Chris hear the mournful baying of a bloodhound in the distance.

But they did notice a police car, which drew up beside them presently, flashing its blue beacon light.

"Good heavens! Ben Jones, whatever are *you* doing out here at this hour of night?" asked the police driver, whose name was Roger Mulvey. He lived in Rainwater Crescent, and his sons Bill and Dave were friends of Chris, and he used to play darts with Mr. Jones on Thursday evenings.

"Some slimy so-and-so pinched my cab and brought it out here," said Mr. Jones. "And now I've been and gone and lost Arabel."

"Well, she's not here—anyone can see that," said Roger Mulvey, shining his flashlight around the huge empty space underneath Rumbury Tower Heights. The moon had risen by now, and it shone clean through from side to side. Nobody was there.

"And *you* can't stay," Roger went on. "My orders are

to warn everybody and get them cleared out of this area."

"Why?" said Mr. Jones rather grumpily. He did not feel that Roger was being as helpful as a policeman ought to be.

"Why? Because the Detective Branch was dragging Rumbury Canal for some reason, and the silly lubbers went and pulled the plug out of the bottom of the canal, and all the water's run away. Like a bath."

"Run away? Where to?"

"Well, these here Rumbury Marshes are the lowest part of the town, so the water's just naturally bound to turn up here before long. Any minute now there'll be a big flood. In fact"—he pointed—"there it comes *now*, so you better get in your cab and scarper."

"But what about Arabel?" Mr. Jones was horrified. "And Mortimer?"

"Well, you can see they aren't here," said Roger, reasonably. "So get a move on!" And he went whizzing off with his blue lights flashing to warn any other people who might be out on Rumbury Marsh in the moonlight.

Now Mr. Jones and Chris could see quite a lot of water pouring across the marsh, shining like icing sugar, so Mr. Jones leaped into his taxi and Chris sprang onto his motorbike, and they, too, shot away to the higher land by the public library and the gas works. And in ten minutes Rumbury Tower Heights, standing on its twelve legs, was marooned in the middle of a great swashing inland sea, twenty feet deep, in which a lot of marshmallows were bobbing about.

Mr. Jones and Chris, nearly mad with worry, could think of nothing better to do than go back to Number Six, Rainwater Crescent, in case by some lucky chance Arabel and Mortimer had managed to get home before them. But of course all they found was Mrs. Jones knitting and having hysterics.

"Mortimer and Arabel's been kidnapped by a Dictionary Gang," she wailed at them. "And Cousin Sam's out dragging the canal for them this very minute, so *you'd* better get a boat and start looking too."

Chris and Mr. Jones gazed at each other glumly. They could get no more sense out of Mrs. Jones (if what she had said so far could be called sense), so her husband put her to bed with a cup of tea and a Dormodol pill.

"My mate Sandy's got a dinghy with an outboard," said Chris thoughtfully. "Maybe Mrs. Jones has got a point. We could borrow Sandy's dinghy and go out on the floods in it, for a look-round."

Mr. Jones could find no fault with this plan, so they went along to the Smith house, which was also in Rainwater Crescent. Mr. Smith was not very pleased at being woken at four in the morning, which it was by now, with a request for his son's dinghy, but when he heard that there was a flood, and that Arabel Jones was missing, he became more helpful.

"Sandy's not here—he's staying the night with a couple of pals of his, Bill and Dave Mulvey—but he'd certainly let you have the boat. It's in the garden—help yourself."

So Chris and Mr. Jones put the boat on top of Mr. Jones's taxi and drove back from Rainwater Crescent toward Rumbury Waste.

4

Meanwhile, what had happened to Mortimer?

He had been very interested indeed to find himself inside Rumbury Tower Heights. Because no one had ever made use of it, the building was not furnished at all. There were hundreds of big empty rooms and long empty passages. There were two elevators in the middle, which were not working because there was no power, and there were escalators, all the way from the first floor to the twentieth, which were also stationary, like ordinary stairs with a smooth handrail on each side. Mortimer had an enjoyable time for half an hour or so climbing up some flights of the escalator and then sliding down the handrail, shouting "Nevermore!" at the top of his voice.

Since the building was not furnished, there were no carpets on the floors or curtains over the windows, it was all bare and echoing, it carried sound particularly well, and Mortimer's shouts rang from the first floor to the twentieth, sounding like the Day of Judgment. This soon disturbed the bats, who had taken up residence on the fourth floor. They began to squeak and flap, and to drop off the picture rails where they were hanging in large black clumps like bunches of grapes, and to fly around the building, going all the way up and down the center well, where the escalator was, and along the passages.

Mortimer became tremendously excited when the bats came out. They were a great deal bigger than he was, with wide leathery wings, long snouts, tiny eyes, sharp teeth, and big complicated ears. They had a claw on each hand, but were not really fierce; they were rather gentle simple creatures who lived on fruit when they could get it, but as they could not get fruit in Rumbury Tower Heights, had to make do with spiders and earwigs. Mortimer was not in the least afraid of the bats, although there were such a lot of them; he began to chase them about, shouting "Nevermore!" He even flew— a thing he was not fond of doing. The poor bats grew very flustered indeed—they had never come across anything like Mortimer—they circled wildly about the building, squeaking and shrilling and flapping their wings with a noise like washing in a high wind.

And this disturbance of the bats had other unexpected results.

The first was that five rather short men in black cloaks and extremely large hats suddenly erupted from a room on the eighth floor and fled in terrible disarray along one of the corridors, shrieking: "*Dio mio! Allegro ma non troppo! Così fan tutte!* Vampires, vampires!" at the tops of their voices.

They passed clean by Arabel without noticing her, in their terror and confusion; Arabel had been going steadily through the building, floor by floor, looking for Mor-

timer in the moonlight that came through the Venetian blinds on the windows. There was such a lot of fuss and commotion going on in the building that she felt sure Mortimer must be somewhere not far off.

The Hatmen—for these five men were the fiendish Mediterranean gang who had kidnapped Naughty Madge Owens—went careering down one of the stationary escalators, tripping, stumbling, and falling over one another. Their progress down the escalator was not helped by the fact that piles of books were stacked on every step. At the bottom, on the seventh floor, they were brought to a stop by a massive rampart of books. Filippo Fedora, the leader of the gang, was in front, and hit the pile of books at such speed that the whole enormous heap toppled over on the rest of the gang as they came barreling down, knocking them all unconscious.

Arabel had not observed this, for she heard a voice crying: "Help! Help!" The voice seemed to be coming from the room out of which the Hatmen had dashed so hastily. Arabel went in, to see who was calling, and there she found Naughty Madge Owens, tied by her hands and legs to a chair, and looking very indignant.

A lot of bats were flying around overhead.

"Shall I untie you?" said Arabel.

"Yes, do, for goodness sake!" said Naughty Madge Owens. She was as skinny as a broom handle, with very pale cheeks, and flashing blue eyes, and extremely white teeth, and a huge mop of shiny black curls, like a bolster on her head. She said: "I want to take off my wig, before the bats nest in it. And I can't do that with my hands tied."

As soon as Arabel had untied her, Madge lifted off the wig, underneath which she had quite short straight hair, about the same length as a wire-haired terrier's. "That's better!" she remarked.

In fact the bats showed no wish to nest in her wig, but, as she said, "You can't be too careful, and that wig cost a fortune."

She put the wig carefully in her enormous handbag.

"Aren't you Naughty Madge Owens?" asked Arabel, who often listened to Rumbury Pirate Radio and watched *Top of the Pops.*

"Yes I am, and I can't *think* why nobody's rescued me before, you'd think *somebody* would have started wondering where I was by now, I was due to sing on Rumbury Radio this evening and dear knows I've enough fans—where are they all?" said Madge Owens, still rather crossly. "Not that I don't mean to say thanks ever so to you, ducks, for I certainly do! Let's get out of here while those rotten skunks of Hatmen are out of the way, shall we?"

"We can go down the fire escape," said Arabel, for a door led out to it from the room where Madge Owens had been imprisoned. But when they stepped out onto the fire escape they were very startled indeed to see that Rumbury Tower Heights was now standing in the middle of a lagoon that shone all misty and silvery in the moonlight.

"Coo!" said Arabel. "It wasn't like that before! I wonder when that happened." And then she said: "Oh dear, I do hope Pa and Chris are all right."

At that moment the attention of Arabel and Madge Owens was attracted by a sound close beside them. What was their surprise and curiosity at seeing three people who were occupied in climbing up the wall of Rumbury Tower Heights! The climbers had pitons, iron pegs which they knocked into the concrete wall and then used to pull themselves up. They all carried large bundles on their backs.

"Hullo, Arabel," said one of them. He proved to be Sandy Smith, from Number Eight, Rainwater Crescent. "What are *you* doing here?" he said.

"What are *you*?" said Arabel.

"Bill and Dave and me are the founder members of the R.C.C., that's the Rumbury Climbers' Club," said Sandy, continuing to climb. "We're going up to the top."

"We'll come and meet you there," said Arabel.

She and Naughty Madge did not use the climbers' pitons to get to the top of the building. They merely walked up the fire escape. By now the pink light of dawn was beginning to creep into the sky. It was a fine view, over the surging flood, toward the public library and the gasworks, with the Town Hall in the background.

A cool wind was blowing, and Madge put her wig back on, as the bats were all downstairs. "I'd certainly like to know why my fans haven't come to rescue me," she said again.

Of course many of her fans, still asleep in bed, did not even know yet that she was missing, but they soon would when they got up and read the headlines in the *Rumbury Daily News*:

POP STAR FAILS TO SHOW

FOR RUMBURY RADIO—

WHERE IS NAUGHTY MADGE?

Sandy, Dave, and Bill had reached the top, pulled a lot of equipment from their packs, and were slotting it together.

"What are those?" asked Arabel.

"Hang gliders," said Sandy. "Bill and Dave and I are founder members of the R.H.G.C.—the Rumbury Hang Gliders' Club. Cor!" he said, gazing at Madge. "Aren't you Naughty Madge Owens? Come on, then, Madgie— give us a song!"

"I will," said Madge, "if you'll give us a lift down in one of those things. Can you take a passenger?"

The three boys looked at each other.

"Never tried," said Sandy.

"*Might* be OK," said Dave.

"No harm in having a bash," said Bill. "After all, they can only go *down*, can't they?"

So they went on fitting their gliders together, and Madge opened her mouth and sang at the top of her tremendously powerful lungs the song that had first got her to Number Two in the charts:

> *"Evil, idle Isidore,*
> *Every day I love him, more and more.*
> *He's evil—he's idle,*
> *Downright homicidal.*
> *He's my guru and my idol,*
> *My love for him is tidal,*
> *He's the only guy that I adore!*
> *Evil, evil, idle, idle Isidore!*
> *Every day I idolize him, more and more.*
> *He's so evil—so idle*
> *That hunting far and wide'll*
> *Never find another guy like Isidore!"*

Madge's voice carried like a peal of bells over the floods. Some people rowing around in boats down below looked up, and began shouting. Some people began to gather along the dry land, over Rumbury Waste.

Meanwhile, what was happening downstairs?

Mortimer had become bored by chasing the bats, and was sitting thoughtfully munching up the OWL to POL volume of the encyclopedia, staring at the Hatmen, who were still lying unconscious among piles of books.

Mortimer was beginning to pine for Arabel, which he did whenever they had been apart for more than a couple of hours.

Suddenly he heard the sound of feet coming up the stairs—one pair of human feet, and the pit-pat of four dog's paws.

Into sight up the stationary escalator came the tall, commanding figure of Miss Acaster, the head librarian. She was being pulled along by a large bloodhound on a lead. The bloodhound was woofling with great excitement and interest, and it made a beeline for the feet of Mr. Beeline, which were sticking out from under a pile of foreign dictionaries. They had fallen on him when the Hatmen hurtled down in their mad descent.

Miss Acaster was surprised at the sight of Mortimer,

and even more so when she noticed all the unconscious Hatmen. But she nodded grimly when the bloodhound dug out Mr. Beeline from his pile of books.

"Caught red-handed, selling his loot to a gang of receivers," she remarked. She had been suspicious of Mr. Beeline for some weeks, having noticed that he always seemed fatter when he left the library than when he entered it.

She had borrowed Rollo, the bloodhound, from her brother, who bred bloodhounds, and used him to track down Mr. Beeline, arriving at Rumbury Tower Heights just five minutes before the flood. Rollo could not possibly have managed the fire escape, but fortunately Miss Acaster's brother was also the architect who built Rumbury Tower Heights, and he had told her about a concealed door in one of the legs that supported the building, and had given her a key. The door opened onto a spiral stair, leading up inside the leg. In fact the Hatmen had got in that way too, and had left the door open, which was lucky for Miss Acaster; she and Rollo just got in before the flood. But it had taken them a long time to toil up the spiral stair.

Now Miss Acaster went around in a businesslike way, checking the piles of books, which were all from Rumbury Library. Then she stapled all the Hatmen to the floor by the wide brims of their hats. (She had brought a staple-gun with her, in case Mr. Beeline turned violent.) While she was doing this, Mr. Beeline began to come to, and peered feebly out from under the dictionaries. He saw Mortimer sitting on the stair rail, and

said venomously: "There! Didn't Mr. Trigg say it was that raven that was stealing the library books?"

"Rubbish, Mr. Beeline," replied Miss Acaster. "You should not try to pin the blame on an innocent bird. I have been following you on my bicycle. Furthermore I saw you tuck *Mrs. Beeton's Household Management* into the waistband of your trousers before you left the library." She tapped the waistband, which gave out a sound like a brick wall. *Mrs. Beeton's Household Management* was still inside. Despite Mr. Beeline's protests, Miss Acaster stapled him to the floor by his trousers and sleeves, alongside the rest of the criminals.

"But I don't know anything about *them*," he protested querulously.

Miss Acaster ignored this. Hearing a lot of noise coming from higher up, she made her way up the escalator by the tumbled piles of books. Mortimer followed her hopefully, for he connected her in his mind with Arabel; they were always handing books to each other.

Sure enough, coming out on the roof, they found Arabel, Naughty Madge Owens, and the three boys.

"Kaaark!" said Mortimer joyfully on seeing Arabel, and he made his way to her as fast as he could without actually flying.

Then he noticed the hang gliders, and was struck dumb with amazement and admiration. They were like nothing he had ever encountered.

"Dear me! Hang gliders—how very convenient," said Miss Acaster. "Could one of you boys take me as a passenger, do you think?"

"Blimey," muttered Bill, "how many *more* passengers are going to come up out of there?" He looked doubtfully at Miss Acaster, so tall and bony, and even more doubtfully at Rollo, who was big and heavy, even for a bloodhound.

Arabel leaned as far as she dared over the parapet, for she thought she could see her father and Chris, down below, coasting over the floods in Dave's dinghy.

"Pa! Chris! I'm up here, with Mortimer!" she called.

Arabel's voice was not very loud, but when Naughty Madge Owens yelled: "Hey, Mr. Jones! Your daughter's up here!" both Chris and Mr. Jones heard her, and waved, beaming.

A great roar of cheering went up also from all the boats, and from the people along Rumbury Wasteside. Papers were waved and ribbons were fluttered. Naughty Madge's fans had arrived.

"Now: Who's going first?" asked Dave.

"I'll take Arabel and Mortimer," said Sandy.

He harnessed himself to his hang glider. Then he buckled his belt around Arabel, passing one end of it through the hang-glider harness. He would have buckled Mortimer also, but Mortimer refused to be buckled.

"I'll just hold him," Arabel said.

"Mind you hold tight, then," said Sandy.

He climbed on the parapet, jumped off, and floated gently down, gliding right across the floods to land on the dry ground in front of the public library.

Everybody cheered like mad.

Then Dave followed with Miss Acaster. He flatly refused to take Rollo, who remained on the roof howling heartbreakingly.

"I'll send somebody back for you right away, Rollo," called Miss Acaster.

Rollo looked and sounded as if he did not believe her.

Dave and Miss Acaster managed to glide even farther than Sandy had with Arabel, perhaps because they were both heavier. They landed by the gasworks. A crowd rushed to welcome them, including some police.

"I shall have to take you into custody, Miss Acaster," said the Chief Constable of Rumbury Town, as he had already to Sandy and Arabel. "The charge is illegal entry of private premises, and operating a hang glider in a built-up area."

Miss Acaster drew herself up to her full height. Her eyes flashed.

She said: "I have been retrieving stolen Council property! You will find a thousand stolen library books inside that building. And I have personally apprehended the thieves; you will find them stapled to the floor. And these young people have been assisting me."

"Stapled to the floor, eh?" said the Chief Constable, scratching his head. He let the prisoners go again.

"Please send somebody over to rescue that blood-hound immediately," ordered Miss Acaster.

Now Bill Mulvey and Naughty Madge Owens came floating to the edge of the flood. This time the cheers were so deafening that the whole of Rumbury town rang and shook and rocked. All her fans rushed to be first to greet Naughty Madge, who would certainly have been trampled to death if the Chief Constable hadn't thrust her into his enormous car.

"Hey! You police weren't a lot of help!" Naughty Madge said tartly to the Chief Constable. "Kidnapped by a gang of mobsters and I didn't see *you* rushing to rescue me!"

"Who did rescue you, then, miss?"

"*She* did," said Naughty Madge, pointing to Arabel, who was being hugged by her father and Chris.

"And where are the miscreants who kidnapped you, then, miss?" said the Chief Constable, who didn't believe a word. He thought it was all a publicity stunt.

"I daresay they are still in that building," said Naughty Madge, adjusting her wig, for a lot of news-paper photographers were taking pictures.

"That building must be packed with criminals like a sardine tin," grumbled the Chief Constable. However he sent a boatful of armed police to investigate.

Arabel, Mortimer, Chris, and Mr. Jones went home to breakfast, returning Sandy's boat on the way. Mrs. Jones had just woken up. She was so pleased to see Arabel and Mortimer that she didn't make as much fuss as they expected; instead she scrambled a whole lot of eggs and made twelve pieces of toast.

The Hatmen were sent to prison.

Mr. Beeline did not go to prison, but was given such a warning that he completely stopped stealing library books, and instead took to pinching police barricades and orange lights from pedestrian crossings.

Rumbury Tower Heights still stands empty, and the bats are still in residence. Dave, Bill, and Sandy plan to have another go at hang gliding from the top some time when the Chief Constable is engaged elsewhere.

Mortimer is very happy. He has ridden on the fountain *and* on a hang glider; even more than he expected.

Naughty Madge Owens sent Arabel a brooch, and a T-shirt with her picture on it, autographed.

And, thank goodness, the trench along Rainwater Crescent has been filled in at last, so that Mr. Jones can park his taxi in front of the house again.

MORTIMER'S CROSS

1

It was a bitterly cold February day. The wind was as sharp as a nutmeg grater. Arabel's socks, when Mrs. Jones pegged them on the line, stopped steaming at once, and hung absolutely stiff, as if they had small stone feet inside them. Mr. Jones, who was a taxi driver, had to spray his taxi with antifreeze before it would start; and besides that, he had to put pots of hot porridge and hot coffee inside the hood. Arabel Jones, even when she was indoors, wore so many sweaters that she looked like a football with two fair pigtails.

The only happy member of the family was Mortimer Jones, the raven. His black feathers were so thick and glossy that no amount of cold weather seemed to make him shiver.

But Mrs. Jones kept saying, "Ohhhh, it is bitter! I can't manage to get warm, not any way. Can't stop shivering." Then, when Mr. Jones came home for his lunch, she said, "My head isn't half hot, Ben. And my insides feel ever so all-overish. I believe I've been and gone and got the flu."

"Oh, bless me, Martha!" he said. "That's awkward, that is. You'd best get into bed, right off, and I'll stay home this afternoon and look after you. But what's to

be done tomorrow? I'm booked to fetch a party of six from Bobbing Key, and take them to see the Radnor-Rumbury soccer match at Twickenham."

"Why don't you ask Auntie Meg to come and look after Ma?" said Arabel, as Mrs. Jones went slowly upstairs to bed, and Mr. Jones waited for a kettle to boil, to make a hot-water bottle.

"That's a real sensible notion, Arabel dearie," said Mr. Jones, and as soon as his wife was settled with her hot bottle and two layers of quilts, he telephoned first the doctor, and then his sister Meg, who helped run a pub on the edge of Wales.

The doctor said he couldn't come till tomorrow early. Rumbury Town was full of people with flu. He was run off his feet, and Mrs. Jones was to stay in bed and take lots of hot lemon and aspirins. Mr. Jones's sister Meg said she was sorry but she couldn't come; her cousin Gwen, who helped her run the pub, was in the hospital with flu and a touch of pleurisy, so Meg had to manage the pub on her own.

"It's a terrible time," she said. "Everyone's got the flu, except the ones that haven't. Why don't you send for Aunt Olwen? *She'd* come like a shot. She *loves* looking after other people's houses, and if a flu germ came up to her she'd hit it with a broom handle."

"Yeah; I reckon I'll have to get her," said Mr. Jones heavily. "Thanks, Meg."

"By the way," said Meg, "there's a box of clothes and toys Martha promised to let me have. For my Friends of Foxhounds Relief Society. I need it urgently for the sale on Thursday. D'you know if Martha sent it off?"

"I dunno," said Mr. Jones. "I seem to remember her packing it up. I'll see. Good-bye, Meg."

Then he telephoned his aunt Olwen in Bangor.

"That you, Ben?" said Aunt Olwen. "Yes. I'll come. Flu, Martha's got, has she? Humph! That's what comes of wearing nylons and that thin underwear. No more than to be expected. Time and again I've said so. Well, you'll all get it now, I daresay. First thing tomorrow morning I'll be with you. My neighbor Tom Griffith can bring me. Driving up to London anyway, he is, to see the soccer match at Twickenham. I'll be in Rumbury Town by breakfast time. And I'll bring sister Bronwen's clock that she left you when she passed on."

"I dunno as we've room for the clock—" Mr. Jones began, but his aunt Olwen had already hung up.

So it was arranged.

When Arabel heard that, instead of cheerful talkative lively Aunt Meg, they were to be looked after by her great-aunt Olwen, she let out a wail of dismay.

"Oh, Pa! Last time Great-aunt was here, she put some stuff on my hair to stop it tangling that made it set as hard as cement. And she made me swallow five spoonfuls of cod-liver oil before every *single* meal. And she spent three days cleaning the house, and two days scrubbing inside the teapot, specially the spout, and then the spout came away in her hand. And she switched off all the switches in the house, so that everything in the deepfreeze went moldy. You said it would be over your dead body if she ever came here again."

"I know, dearie, but it'll be over your ma's dead body if she *don't* come," said Mr. Jones, poking his fingers through his hair till it looked like a bunch of windblown chrysanthemums.

"And Great-aunt Olwen's never even seen Mortimer,

because we didn't have him last time she came," Arabel went on anxiously, looking at the raven, who had piled a foot-high mound of tea bags on the lid of the washing machine, and was trying to stand on his head on top of the pile. He was the wrong shape for standing on his head, and each time he tried, he fell heavily on his back, and the tea bags flew all over the kitchen floor. They were getting rather dusty. Mr. Jones supposed he ought to stop Mortimer, but he had too much else on his mind.

"It would certainly be a good thing if Aunt Olwen *didn't* see Mortimer, lovey," he said. "You don't suppose, just while she's here, that you could ask Mortimer to stay inside his box?"

Mortimer's box stood in a corner of the kitchen by

the refrigerator. Auntie Meg had once brought it up, when she came on a visit, full of Worcester apples. Arabel and Mortimer both liked the box because it had MORTIMER'S CROSS stenciled on its side, and under that the letters H.A.R.R.I.S. A long time ago the box had held a lot of sockets, which were being delivered to the Hereford Admiralty Radar Research and Information Station, and then it had held empty beer bottles, which the men who worked at the Mortimer's Cross Radar Station were taking back to the pub, and then Auntie Meg had used it for apples. Arabel said that the letters H.A.R.R.I.S. stood for *Hush! A Resting Raven's Inside, Ssh!* Ever since the box had come into the house, Mortimer had used it as a brooding-place. At times when he was sulky, or gloomy, or upset, or thoughtful, or wanted to remember something, or digest his lunch, or

just go to sleep, he climbed into the box, and pulled the four flaps down over his head. Sometimes, in cold or wet weather, he stayed there for hours.

Arabel looked thoughtfully at the box now, and said, "I could *ask* him. But the trouble is, if you ask Mortimer to do something, it mostly makes him want to do something else, just the opposite."

"You're telling me," said Mr. Jones. "Oh well, have to hope for the best, I suppose." He did not *sound* at all hopeful.

Next day was colder than ever. Great-aunt Olwen arrived before breakfast. She and Mr. Griffith had been driving all night, in his big old car that only went forty miles an hour. Mr. Griffith said the roads were like frozen salad oil. Great-aunt Olwen wore a black bugled dolman all covered with jet beads, a bonnet with forty shining black cherries on it, black high-button boots, and a big black shawl that covered her from head to foot and made her look like a walking wigwam. She had an umbrella, and a chimney-sweep's brush, and a Gladstone bag, which contained six white aprons, an alarm clock, a flannel nightgown, an electric scrubbing-brush, a four-pound tin of beeswax, a carton of Best Cardiff Scouring Powder, and a window-cleaning tool. They also had with them in the car Mr. Griffith's Saint Bernard, Sam, and Great-aunt Olwen's sister Bronwen's grandfather clock, which was six feet high, so it was lucky the car was a big one. The mahogany case of the clock was decorated all over with brown and gold birds and fishes. The clock face had the sun, moon, stars, and

a rainbow on it. Arabel thought it very beautiful. The clock's door swung open as Mr. Jones and Mr. Griffith were carrying it into the house, staggering rather, because it was so heavy. The clock door was three feet above ground level, where the clock's stomach might have been; inside could be seen a big brass pendulum, which swung slowly from side to side, and two large iron weights dangling on cords.

Mortimer, who had been sitting on the windowsill halfway up the stairs, half hidden by the curtain, stared very hard at the clock's inside. He was disappointed when Mr. Jones shut the door and turned the key.

"Phew!" said Mr. Griffith, wiping his forehead. "Good riddance to get rid of that, I'm telling you. Struck every blessed quarter from Bangor to here; and a tick loud enough to drown nightingales. Where d'you want her, Ben?"

"Right here in the hall is the only place where there's room," said Mr. Jones, who was anxious to settle his aunt and hurry off to pick up his customers in Bobbing Key. "And thank you kindly, Tom Griffith, for taking the trouble to bring it; not to mention my auntie Olwen."

"No trouble," said Mr. Griffith. "Coming up from Bangor anyway. But as for *that* one—"

Great-aunt Olwen had already stumped off upstairs, switching on her hearing aid as she went. She did not notice Mortimer behind his curtain. But he was mightily interested in her hearing aid, and peered at it as she went by.

Mr. Griffith threw up his eyes, shook his head after Great-aunt Olwen, and hissed, "Proper cockatrice you've got there, my word! Make a pterodactyl go back and wipe its feet on the mat, *she* would. Wanted my Sam to run behind the car, all the way from Bangor."

Mr. Griffith's Saint Bernard was looking in the front door with great mournful Saint Bernard eyes. His ears, the size of dishcloths, hung down on either side of his face. "Said she wasn't used to traveling with a dog that size in the car, and if he was used to following tracks, he might as well follow ours."

"Is he used to following tracks, Mr. Griffith?" asked Arabel.

"Follow a mosquito from here to the moon, dearie."

At this moment Mortimer came flopping down the stairs, and, after quietly edging close to Sam, suddenly took hold of the Saint Bernard's tail. There was a short, sharp scene. Then Mr. Griffith and Sam went off to have breakfast at the Eggs-Quiz-It Snackbar, and Mr. Jones hurried away to pick up his fares in Bobbing Key.

"You shouldn't have done that to Sam, Mortimer," said Arabel. "He was a visitor."

Mortimer took no notice. He was staring thoughtfully at the grandfather clock. But Mr. Jones, knowing Mortimer's habits, had taken out the key and put it in his waistcoat pocket.

In a couple of hours, Great-aunt Olwen had the house turned upside down.

First she moved all the furniture in Mrs. Jones's bedroom "so as to make it easier to get at the patient."

While she had four chairs, the laundry basket, an electric heater, and a standard lamp piled on the wardrobe, which lay on its side, the front doorbell rang.

"I expect that's the doctor," said Arabel, peering into her mother's room over a barricade of furniture.

"What did you say, dear?" said Great-aunt Olwen, turning up her hearing aid.

Great-aunt Olwen's hearing aid consisted of a plug, which fitted her ear, a cord, which dangled round her neck, and, at the other end of the cord, a little box with

a battery inside it and a grating on the front. It had a switch like a radio so that the volume could be turned up or down. The box was pinned to Aunt Olwen's apron bib. When the grating was turned toward a sound, Aunt Olwen could hear it; but Arabel was standing behind her great-aunt.

"Speak up, child!" said Great-aunt Olwen, turning up the hearing aid a bit more.

"There's someone at the front door. I expect it's the doctor!" shouted Arabel, climbing over the wardrobe and coming round to the front of her great-aunt.

"No need to shout, child, I can hear you perfectly well. I'm not deaf! Answer the door, then, will you, while I just vacuum under your mother's bed," said Great-aunt Olwen, poking the nozzle of the vacuum cleaner under poor Mrs. Jones.

Arabel climbed back over the wardrobe and went to answer the front door.

Outside was Dr. McCaution, looking harassed.

"Mrs. Jones, Number Six, Rainwater Crescent, says she has flu," he muttered, looking at his list, which was as long as the Trans-Siberian Railway.

"Will you come upstairs, please?" said Arabel.

As the doctor went ahead of her up the stairs he noticed the sound of the grandfather clock ticking. It had an exceptionally loud tick-tock, tick-tock, very slow and solemn; it sounded like an ostrich, with iron weights tied to its feet, crossing a hollow glass pavement. And Mortimer, sitting in front of the clock, was grumbling to himself vexedly between ticks, so what the doctor heard went like this:

"Tick. Nevermore. Tock. Nevermore. Tick. Nevermore. Tock. *Kaaark!*"

"Advise you to put a stop to *that*," said the doctor. "Disturbing for an invalid, very; in fact it's enough to *give* anybody flu—if not delirium tremens—just listening to it."

He was obliged to shove away the wardrobe lying on its side across the doorway of Mrs. Jones's room; then he gazed around him in surprise. The bedroom was looking very upheaved; all the curtains, the bedcover, and the frilly skirts of the dressing table were piled on the towel rail; the carpet was rolled up, and every bit of furniture was on top of something else. Great-aunt Olwen had finished vacuuming (although she had not switched the cleaner off); she was about to scrub; Dr. McCaution only just avoided putting his foot in a pail of hot soapy water.

"God bless my soul, ma'am, what's this, stocktaking day or Judgment Day?" said the doctor, putting a thermometer into Mrs. Jones's mouth and taking her pulse.

"Cleanliness, young man, is next to godliness," said Great-aunt Olwen.

"What the blue blazes is making that buzzing noise?" said the doctor.

As well as the noise of the vacuum cleaner, there was a harsh rattling buzz coming from one corner of the room.

"Oh, d-d-doctor! Maybe it's me! Maybe I've got the d-death-rattles," whimpered poor Mrs. Jones, taking the thermometer out of her mouth and putting it into a cup of hot lemon that Arabel had brought her.

"Rubbish, Mrs. Jones; it's coming from that Gladstone bag."

Great-aunt Olwen's bag stood near the door. She had not completely unpacked it yet, she had been so eager to get to the cleaning; had only taken out the beeswax, the window-cleaning tool, the scouring powder, and the first of her six white aprons. There was an unmistakable loud buzz coming from the bag. Aunt Olwen had not noticed it because her hearing aid was not very good at distinguishing one buzz from another.

"Maybe it's a bomb," suggested Arabel.

Dr. McCaution approached the bag with care. Then he turned it sharply upside down, scattering the contents.

"Mind what you do with other people's property, young man!" said Great-aunt Olwen.

The noise proved to have been Great-aunt Olwen's electric battery-operated scrubbing brush, which had been whirring away to itself all the way up from Bangor.

Mr. Griffith had not heard it because the grandfather clock had been ticking so loudly. The scrubbing-brush did a kind of dance, all by itself, over the bare boards; then the battery ran out, and it stopped.

"There! I must have forgotten to switch it off, and now the battery's worn out," said Great-aunt Olwen. "Ben will have to get a new one. I'm *that* absentminded, one of these days I'll forget to breathe."

Mrs. Jones looked as if she hoped that day would come soon.

The doctor pulled the thermometer out of the cup of hot lemon and looked at it.

"You've got flu, Mrs. Jones," he said, scribbling on his pad. "You have a temperature of a hundred and thirty-six. Take these pills eight times a day, stay in bed till I tell you to get up, and *complete* rest and quiet, please; no noise or disturbances. Invalids need a peaceful, re-laxed atmosphere," he shouted at Great-aunt Olwen, who had fetched her window-cleaning tool and was squeaking it up and down the dressing-table glass. The vacuum cleaner was still roaring to itself, and Great-aunt Olwen's hearing aid, turned up to full volume, was letting out a high whine. "Anybody can see *this* hasn't been touched for months," she muttered grimly, wiping the glass with a washcloth, taking no notice of the doctor.

Now from downstairs there came a tremendous clanging chime. It went on and on, sixteen strokes for the four quarters, then ten strokes for the hour.

"Good gad, what's that?" said the doctor, looping his muffler around his neck.

"It's my husband's mother's grandfather clock," whispered Mrs. Jones faintly. "Aunt Olwen just brought it from Bangor."

"Worth a mint, that clock is," said Aunt Olwen with satisfaction. Even she had heard the chimes.

"It's louder than the Concorde," said the doctor. "You could get middle-ear disturbance listening to it. Better stick a sock in its stomach while you've got illness in the house. See you tomorrow, Mrs. Jones."

Great-aunt Olwen followed Arabel and the doctor downstairs because she wanted some mothballs to tuck in between the bedclothes.

Down in the front hall, the first thing she saw was Mortimer. He had pulled the piano stool across the dining room, out into the hall, and up against the clock; he had hoisted the coal scuttle on top of the stool, and was now standing on the coal, with his eye pressed to the keyhole of the clock door.

"What in the world is *that*?" said Great-aunt Olwen sharply.

Her voice startled Mortimer. The coal scuttle was not very well balanced on the piano stool, and when Mortimer turned around, he and the scuttle fell off the stool, thumping heavily against the door of the clock, and strewing coal over the gray wall-to-wall carpet.

The clock began striking as if all the hours had been joined together between now and the year two thousand.

"Oh, mercy, mercy, what's happened, stop that awful noise!" wailed Mrs. Jones from upstairs. "My head feels as if it's going to split in half like a coconut."

The doctor kicked the clock till it stopped striking, and then escaped from Number Six, Rainwater Crescent, shouting, "Get that prescription made up as soon as possible!"

Mortimer had fallen among the lumps of coal, and was just picking himself up. Disappointed in his plan for getting into the clock, he was now gazing very keenly at Great-aunt Olwen's hearing aid.

"What's *that*?" said Great-aunt Olwen again. She had fetched a brush and pan, and was sweeping up the coal. She poked at Mortimer with the brush.

"That's Mortimer," said Arabel. "He's our raven."

"Raven, you call him? He looks to me like a black imp from the pit," said Great-aunt Olwen. "Into a bath he goes

before I'm an hour older, or my name's not Olwen
Gwladys Angharad Merlwyn Jones. Crawling with germs
from head to toe, he is, without a shadow of doubt; no
wonder Martha has the flu, only surprising it isn't pleurisy, psittacosis, and Ponsonby's disease."

"Oh, please, I don't think Mortimer would like being
bathed at all, he isn't used to that sort of thing," said
Arabel.

"He'll be used to it soon," said Aunt Olwen ominously,
making a grab for Mortimer.

In return he made a snatch for her hearing aid, but
only succeeded in unplugging the cord from the box
holding the battery.

"You just wait, you Turk!" threatened Great-aunt
Olwen.

Luckily, at this moment, Mrs. Jones's sister Brenda
rang the doorbell; Mr. Jones had told her Martha had
flu, and she had come to ask if there was any way in
which she could help, apart from staying in the house,
which she could not do, as her husband and two of her
three daughters were coming down with flu too.

Great-aunt Olwen gave her the prescription to take
to the pharmacy, and she took Arabel along with her to
carry the basket. Arabel did not want to go; she was
anxious about Mortimer; but he had retired into his
box, and she hoped he would be safe there. Great-aunt
Olwen had not noticed him getting in.

Unfortunately for lunch they had tomato soup and
biscuits. Mortimer loved tomato soup. He came out of
the box while Aunt Olwen was upstairs taking Mrs. Jones

some camomile tea. She had made it with ginger by mistake, and Mrs. Jones didn't much fancy it.

"Please, Mortimer, I think it would be best if you got back into your box," Arabel said in a low voice.

Mortimer took no notice. He was drinking a cup of tomato soup, very splashily. And he wanted another look at Great-aunt Olwen's hearing aid.

When Great-aunt Olwen came downstairs again, she gave a sharp look at Mortimer. Then she filled a large tub with hot water and put it on the kitchen table. And she fetched soap, and the vacuum cleaner, and detergent, and pumice stone, and a bottle of disinfectant, and a corkscrew, and a skewer.

"Now then, you!" she said grimly.

"Oh, *please* don't do whatever you're going to do to Mortimer!" cried Arabel in horror. "He won't like it a bit, truly he won't!"

"No nasty germy bird is going to stay in any house that *I'm* in," said Aunt Olwen, pressing her lips tight together.

First she vacuumed Mortimer from head to tail. Twice his head got stuck up the tube, and she hauled him out again by his feet; his feathers stood on end like the rays of the sun, and several of them came out. He was so stunned by this treatment that he had no breath even to protest; anyway most of his breath had been sucked out of him by the vacuum.

Then Great-aunt Olwen plunged Mortimer (whom she was holding by his neck and legs) into the tubful of hot, sudsy water.

There was a terrific commotion. Water and froth rained all over the kitchen. Upstairs, Mrs. Jones called faintly, "Oh, help! Whatever is going on? Is it a Martian invasion? I think I'm going to have a spasm!"

Smothered in soap, Mortimer became too slippery to hold, and he burst upstairs like a steam-propelled missile, leaving a trail of spray and feathers behind him. He did not generally use his wings for flying, but this was one of the times when he thought it best to do so.

In the kitchen, Great-aunt Olwen, replugging her hearing aid, was saying, "He needn't think I'm finished with him yet; just wait till I get my hands on him again."

Mrs. Cross, from down the road, had popped her head around the back door with a bunch of grapes for Arabel's mother. She said to Great-aunt Olwen, "Better let me bandage your hands first." Great-aunt Olwen was bleeding from several peck marks. "I'd leave that bird alone if I were you," advised Mrs. Cross. "He's nothing but trouble."

Great-aunt Olwen had never been defeated yet; she was determined to deal with Mortimer and stop him spreading germs. As soon as she was bandaged, she followed him to the linen closet, where he had taken refuge, and dragged him out from among the sopping towels.

"You're going to have a proper clean-up, whether you like it or not," she told him. She had refilled the tub with hot water and put on heavy cleaning gloves; now she scrubbed Mortimer all over, working the soap in between his feathers with a corkscrew, cleaning his feet with a skewer, and rinsing them separately in a soup plate full of Dyegerm. When Mortimer opened his beak to gasp "Nevermore!" she poked in a piece of soap the size of a butter bean, and Mortimer swallowed it before he could stop himself; after that, whenever he opened his beak to say something, all that came out was clots of froth as big as Ping-Pong balls.

"That'll clean you up inside as well," Great-aunt Olwen said.

Mortimer became quite dazed by all this unexpected misfortune; he no longer even tried to grab Great-aunt Olwen's hearing aid, but just endured what was happening to him. He had gone absolutely stiff, hunching his head down between his shoulder blades, and hugging his wings tightly to his sides. His eyes were shut, so as to keep out the soap.

In the fracas the cord of Aunt Olwen's hearing aid had broken, so she took off the whole contraption and put it on the dresser.

"Ben will have to mend it when he comes in," she said. "Now: that bird's a bit more fit to live in a decent house. Arabel, you take this old bit of towel and dry him; then he can go in front of the stove to finish off. Mercy sakes, look at the time; your mother ought to have had her pill two hours ago."

Great-aunt Olwen fetched her spare hearing aid from her bag, and put on her third apron (two had already been used up); she threw the tubful of Mortimer's bath-water out the back door, where it immediately froze all over the concrete path. Then, still being a bit distracted by all the excitement of cleaning Mortimer, she filled Mrs. Jones's hot-water bottle with lemonade, and took her a cup of hot disinfectant with honey in it; and she gave Arabel fried celery and bacon with salad dressing on it for tea. Great-aunt Olwen was so hasty in all her actions that very often two or three of them got crossed over like this. She put on the spare hearing aid back to front, with its grating pressed against her chest, so all she could hear was her own heart beating.

Mortimer did not want any tea, though Arabel offered him some bacon with salad dressing on it; he turned his head the other way. And when she came to sit by him in front of the warm stove, he opened his eyes, just for a moment, and looked at her almost as if he hated her.

He opened his beak, but all that came out was a ball

of froth, so he shut it again. But Arabel knew what he would have liked to say: *Why didn't you stop that person doing those terrible things to me?*

"It wasn't my fault, Mortimer," Arabel whispered miserably. "I *did* warn you to stay in your box. And I did *try* to stop her."

Mortimer closed his eyes as if he didn't believe her.

Great-aunt Olwen went upstairs to give the guest room a thorough turn-out before making up a bed for herself with clean sheets.

When Mortimer was more or less dry, he climbed slowly and wearily into his MORTIMER'S CROSS box, and pulled the flaps down over himself. Inside the box he had an old piece of blanket, which was comfortably covered with cake crumbs and moldy bits of cheese rind, and dead leaves, and twigs, and snail shells, and dried worms, and Coke-can pop tops, and ice-cream papers, and other things he had collected at one time or another, besides an inch-thick layer of dust; he wrapped himself tight in this blanket, and stuffed his head under his wing. He felt horrible; slimy and itchy between his feathers, damp and uncomfortable under his wings and tail; his feet were sore from the disinfectant, and his eyes stung from the detergent; the soap tasted disgusting in his beak; and even far down under his wing, his feathers smelt of Cleanol.

If there had been a prize going for the most miserable bird in Rumbury Town, Mortimer would certainly have won it.

Mr. Jones became worried when he got back home (which was not very early, because after the soccer match, in which Radnor Forest won the Cup, he had to take his customers back to Bobbing Key). When he let himself in he noticed at once that the house smelt frighteningly clean, of soap and detergent and beeswax and disinfectant; he could hear the loud gloomy tick of the grandfather clock, but, apart from that, no other sound at all.

"Hallo? Where is everybody?" he called.

His aunt Olwen came out of the kitchen.

"Is that you, Ben? Martha's a little better; the doctor said her temperature was a hundred and thirty-six this morning, but it's only a hundred and three now. Don't go up to see her till you've had a good wash, and gargled with Dyegerm; you'll find a big bottle by the kitchen sink. I daresay the whole of outdoors is swarming with germs."

"Where's Arabel?" asked Mr. Jones uneasily. "And—and Mortimer?"

"The child's in her room," snapped Aunt Olwen. "I told her to play with the button box. At my age I can't have children underfoot when I'm trying to get the house cleaned up. As for the bird, he took himself off somewhere, I'm sure I don't know where. And the longer he stays out of sight, the better I'm pleased. Birds in the house, indeed! Now your supper's ready, Ben, so hurry up and eat it."

The supper Aunt Olwen had cooked for Mr. Jones showed signs of her absentmindedness. Instead of stewing apples and grilling hamburgers, she had toasted the apples under the grill, and poached the hamburgers in hot water. Mr. Jones ate them without grumbling. What else could he do? Someone had to look after his wife, Martha, while she had the flu. Afterward he went up to see her. She was hot and feverish.

"The tick of that great clock downstairs goes through my head like a laser beam of Ancient Rome, Ben," she whispered fretfully. "And has it *got* to chime so often? It seems to keep ding-donging away every ten minutes. It's driving me clean dementiated. And where's Arabel? She hasn't been in to see me since teatime. And what about Mortimer? He's ever so quiet. That's never a good sign, you know it isn't. I only hope he's not up to something."

Mr. Jones hoped so too. He knew that when Mortimer was quiet, it did often mean that he was thoughtfully munching up the gas boiler, or dropping eggs off the top of the wardrobe to see how many bounced, or pouring weedkiller into the television.

"I'll see what Mortimer's up to," he said, "and send Arabel to sit with you."

Arabel came to sit by her mother, but she was very pale and quiet.

"What's the matter, dearie?" whispered Mrs. Jones. "Do you think you're coming down with the flu too?"

"No, Ma," said Arabel. "It's just that—" She gulped. "M-Mortimer won't speak to me. Or look at me."

"Why ever not? You've never quarreled with him?" Mrs. Jones was amazed.

"No, Ma. It's because Great-aunt Olwen washed him."

"*Washed* him?"

"And he thinks it was my fault."

"Oh my gracious cats alive!"

Downstairs, Mr. Jones was having the same sort of conversation with his aunt Olwen.

He had stopped the grandfather clock, at ten to seven, by taking the key from his pocket, unlocking the door, bringing the brass pendulum to a stop, and clipping the cords of the two iron weights together with a clothespin, so that they could not move up and down. Aunt Olwen watched all this with a disapproving eye.

"Never been known to stop, that clock hasn't," she said. "Even when my dear sister Bronwen, that was your mother, went to her rest. All the drive up from Bangor it went on ticking—as steady as Saturday. And now you have to stop it!"

"It's driving Martha crazy. And Mrs. Walters from three doors down came to complain about the chime."

"Some people are never grateful," said Aunt Olwen, clamping her lips together.

Mr. Jones peered through the slit in the box beside

the fridge. There was Mortimer, a tight cocoon of greasy, crumby blanket, quiet as the stone inside a Victoria plum, with not a feather showing.

Rather cautiously, Mr. Jones asked his aunt: "Has Mortimer—er—did he behave himself while I was out?"

"Behave himself? I should hope so," snorted Aunt Olwen. "No raven misbehaves himself in any house where I am! I gave him a good scrub, and disinfected him. Disgraceful state that bird was in! *Christmas-pudding crumbs*, I found, in among his feathers. Last year's, for all I know."

"You washed him?" said Mr. Jones faintly. "Washed Mortimer?"

"Indeed I did. All over. Walking parcel of germs, that bird was. No wonder Martha caught the flu."

"Oh dear," said Mr. Jones. It seemed wrong to complain, since Aunt Olwen had come all the way from Bangor to look after them, but he did think that washing Mortimer might have been a terrible mistake.

On his way back upstairs he stopped by Mortimer's box once more.

"Er—I believe she meant it for the best, Mortimer, my boy," he said pleadingly. "I—I expect you'll feel the benefit of it in a few days."

Mr. Jones did not observe that the grandfather clock key fell out from his waistcoat pocket as he stooped over the box. Dead silence came from between the flaps. Not the faintest *Kark*, or whisper of *Nevermore*. Not so much as a bubble of foam, even.

2

Nobody slept well in the Jones house that night. Mrs. Jones tossed and turned in her fever; she twisted about in bed, and cried out, and dreamed that she was posting parcels full of foxhounds to the Hunt Master General, and that Mortimer was being chased by a pack of grandfather clock patients from the watch hospital on Rumbury Hill. Mr. Jones slept on the sofa in the sitting room, so as not to disturb his wife; his feet stuck out over the end, and were soon like lumps of ice. Arabel got out of bed as soon as her father had said good night to her, and spent the next eight hours making a huge pattern with shirt buttons all over her bedroom floor. She cried a good deal as she was doing it. Great-aunt Olwen also slept badly, but that was because of her alarm clock. It had a tremendously loud ring, so that she could hear it even after she had taken off her spare hearing aid for the night; and she set it to go off every hour, so that she could go and look at Mrs. Jones. Every time the alarm went off, it woke everybody else in the house too; those who were asleep, that is.

"Why do you keep coming to look at me, Aunt Olwen?" Mrs. Jones whispered fretfully at three in the morning. "I'm not likely to run away!"

"Coming to see if you're all right, I am," said Aunt Olwen.

"Well I'm *not* all right—I had a horrible dream. Oh, my dear gracious—that reminds me—"

"Reminds you of what?"

"I promised to send a parcel of clothes and books and toys to Ben's sister Meg. For her Friends of Foxhounds

Relief Society sale—and she wants it by Thursday—I
meant to have sent it off two days ago, oh my good
heavens, and Meg is waiting for it, oh dear, oh me—"

"Now don't get into a fidget, Martha, and thrash about
so," said Aunt Olwen. "Maybe Ben mailed it. And if he
didn't, there's nothing that can be done at this time of
night. If it's still there, I'll send it off for you in the
morning."

"By express!"

"Very well, if you're so set on it," said Aunt Olwen,
sucking in her mouth sourly. "Though why you should
waste your money—or Ben's, rather—on friends of
Megan Jones's foxhounds, I'm sure *I* don't know—"

"Downstairs," whispered Mrs. Jones. "In the lounge,
or maybe the kitchen. A big cardboard box. Addressed
to Miss Jones at the Red Dragon, Mortimer's Cross."

"All right, all right, I'll see to it," grumbled Aunt
Olwen. "I didn't get up at three in the morning to worry
about Megan Jones's foxhounds society."

"You will send it the quickest way, won't you?"

"Yes, yes, if you're so set on it," said Aunt Olwen, and
she went back to bed.

Next day Mr. Jones found the atmosphere, and the
breakfast, in Number Six, Rainwater Crescent so dismal
that he went off to drive his taxi at half-past seven in
the morning, and picked up a fare who wanted to be
taken to Stratford-on-Avon. So he was away until after
lunch. Arabel went back to her own room after breakfast, which was porridge with a lot of mysterious black

things in it. Great-aunt Olwen had left the porridge cooking on the stove all night. Arabel wondered if the black things were lumps of coal. Politely, when Great-aunt Olwen wasn't looking, she put them in the sink disposal unit. She spent the morning going on with her button pattern. She looked very pale and hollow eyed.

Mrs. Jones asked about her parcel at lunchtime, when she was sipping a little broth, which tasted as if it had been made from Dark Tan shoe polish.

"Don't fret so, Martha, I sent it off express, just like you asked. Took it to that place on the corner, calls himself Johnny Jardine's Do-or-Die Delivery Agency. He said he'd send a lad on a motorbike with it directly, and it would get there by tomorrow at latest. *Shocking* price it was—four pounds fifty! All for those friends of foxhounds. Ridiculous waste of cash, I call it," sniffed Aunt Olwen.

Mrs. Jones was so relieved at hearing this that she went to sleep quite peacefully, and when the doctor called, her temperature had come down a little.

Mr. Jones came home in the middle of the afternoon, and was pleased to hear that his wife had taken some broth. "And where's Arabel?" he inquired.

"Still up in her room," said Aunt Olwen shortly.

Mr. Jones went up to see his daughter. He discovered that, all across the floor of her room, using hundreds and thousands of shirt buttons, she had made an enormous pearly pattern that said I'M SORRY, MORTIMER, over and over, about eighty times.

"Do you think he'll understand that, Pa?" she said.

"Well—I dunno," Mr. Jones said. He added, trying to sound hopeful about it, "Very likely he will. We never did ask him if he could read. I'll just fetch him up now, shall I, and we'll soon see."

He went downstairs again, into the kitchen, and came to a sudden stop.

"Aunt Olwen—where's Mortimer?"

"Don't ask *me!*" snapped his aunt. "Where would he usually be, at this time of day? Wherever that is, that's where he'll be!"

"He'd most likely be in his box; the one that used to stand here. Where have you put it, Aunt Olwen?"

And Mr. Jones pointed to the space beside the refrigerator, where Mortimer's box usually stood.

"That box? Why, I put a bit of string around it and sent it off. Martha was carrying on about it, like something possessed, at three o'clock in the morning."

"You sent it off?" said Mr. Jones faintly. "Sent it off where?"

"Wherever the address on it said. *I* didn't address it, Martha did. To your blessed sister Megan's friends of foxes something society."

Mr. Jones leaped toward the stairs, then stopped himself. He went into the sitting room and lifted out a large box full of clothes from behind the sofa.

"Aunt Olwen—*this* was the box that ought to have been sent. See, it has Megan's address on a label."

"Well you don't have to hold it under my *nose*; I can *read*," said Aunt Olwen. "And you don't have to shout either, I'm not deaf! That's a daft place to leave a parcel, if you ask me, behind the sofa."

She was beginning to look rather fidgety.

"So you must have sent off *Mortimer*'s box. With him inside it!"

Arabel had come downstairs to see why her father was taking so long in fetching Mortimer. She arrived just in time to hear this. She went as white as a meringue.

"Oh, Pa!" she whispered. "Whatever shall we do?"

"Well, now," said Mr. Jones, "the first thing we must do is not get in a panic." He said this because he was fairly near panic himself. He knew how attached his daughter was to Mortimer. And he didn't want his wife upset. And she did get upset very easily.

He said, "We don't know for *sure* that Mortimer was in that box. So first we'll have a good, quiet hunt all over the house. And the second thing is not to worry your ma; we won't tell her about this, eh, till she's a bit better. And I daresay Aunt Olwen won't mind sending off the *other* box, as she's very good at sending boxes," he added rather coldly. Aunt Olwen gave him an old-fashioned look, but she took the other box, put on her shawl and bonnet, and hurried off. Arabel noticed that there seemed to be something odd about Aunt Olwen's bonnet—most of the cherries seemed to be missing—but Aunt Olwen skewered it on her head and went off without observing this.

While she was out, Mr. Jones and Arabel searched feverishly all over the house for Mortimer. It was easy to do this, because the house was now in such apple-pie order that even the spoons and forks were laid out in rows, like Olympic swimmers; and a large raven anywhere would have been perfectly conspicuous. But no raven was to be seen anywhere; not in the bath, nor the refrigerator, nor the clock, nor the oven, nor the deep-freeze; nowhere.

Aunt Olwen came back from Johnny Jardine's Do-or-Die Delivery Agency, saying, "Well, there's no call to get in such a fuss, Ben. The young man at the office has it down in his dispatch book that the parcel I took him this morning was simply addressed to Mortimer's Cross, H.A.R.R.I.S. So that's where it'll go."

"But that's the Hereford Admiralty Research Station. What'll they do when they open a box and find Mortimer?"

"Don't ask me," said Aunt Olwen shortly. "One thing,

they won't find any germs on him, that I do know. Look here! Look at my bonnet! What's happened to it? Where's all the cherries off it?"

Mr. Jones didn't answer. He went to the telephone and asked for Directory Inquiries.

Aunt Olwen began mixing bran and raisins and chutney, muttering, "Martha needs building up, I'll make an apple crumble. Ben!" she called. "Ben! Where does Martha keep cooking apples?"

"I want the number of Mortimer's Cross Admiralty Research Station, Hereford," Mr. Jones told the operator. "In the larder," he called to Aunt Olwen.

"In the garden? That's a funny place to keep apples," said Aunt Olwen.

"Just wait a minute," said the operator to Mr. Jones.

After he had waited quite a long time, the operator told him that it was a restricted number, and could not be given to ordinary members of the public.

"Who do you wish to contact at that number? And why do you want it?" she said.

"Because," said Mr. Jones, "I have reason to believe that my raven, Mortimer, has been sent there by mistake."

"I beg your pardon? I didn't quite catch what you said."

Mr. Jones began to repeat what he had said, but was distracted by a crash and a loud shriek from the direction of the back door. "Oh blimey, *now* what," he muttered. "Never mind, dear, I'll have to call you back," he said to the operator.

There was nothing in the kitchen to account for the crash and the shriek. But when Mr. Jones looked outside the back door, he saw his aunt Olwen lying flat on the path. She had slipped on the sheet of ice that had formed when she threw out Mortimer's bathwater, and it seemed highly probable that she had broken her leg.

"Don't you move, Aunt Olwen," said Mr. Jones, gritting his teeth, "I'll just run next door and fetch Chris Cross. He's a strong lad, and with the two of us we'll soon have you off there."

Luckily Chris was at home, and he helped Mr. Jones carry Aunt Olwen in and lay her on the sofa; then Mr. Jones phoned for an ambulance, which said it would be there as soon as it could. People were falling down on sheets of ice all over Rumbury Town and the ambulances were running about like ants. Aunt Olwen sucked her mouth in furiously; she knew she could not blame anyone else for the ice, since it was entirely her own fault.

Mr. Jones packed a bag with his aunt's flannel nightdress and toothbrush, since it seemed almost certain that she would have to spend the night in the hospital. He did not put in her six white aprons or the electric scrubber or the window-cleaning tool. "Mind you put in my spare hearing aid that you mended, Ben," she said. "I daresay those young things of nurses all mumble so you can't hear what they say, and I like to be on the safe side."

But the spare hearing aid could not be found. "I left it on the dresser after I mended it," said Mr. Jones. "Maybe Arabel moved it. Arabel, dearie! Where are you? ARABEL!!"

But no answer came from Arabel. After a minute or two Mr. Jones realized, with utter horror, that he was alone in the house with two people, one with flu, and the other a broken leg, while his daughter and his raven were both missing.

Where, meanwhile, *was* Arabel?

While Mr. Jones was out fetching Chris Cross, there had been a ring at the front doorbell. Arabel went to the door and found Mr. Griffith. His large car was parked just along the road with Sam the Saint Bernard looking out.

Mr. Griffith said, "Called to inquire if your great-auntie wanted a ride back to Bangor. I'm just on my way."

"Oh, I *wish* she did," said Arabel sadly. "But she's broken her leg and has to have it mended."

Mr. Griffith brightened up when he heard that Aunt Olwen would not be his passenger. He said, "Your auntie Meg mentioned something about a box of clothes for her Friends of Foxhounds Society. (Can't think why foxhounds need friends, Saint Bernards get on all right without, eh, Sam?) I said, if your ma hadn't sent off the box already, I'd take it, as I'll be going through Mortimer's Cross."

"You *will?*" said Arabel, all excited. "It's all right about the box, Mr. Griffith, Aunt Olwen sent it off. But—if you're going through Mortimer's Cross—could you take *me?* I can stay the night with Auntie Meg—"

"Want you out of the way, do they, while your Ma's sick?" said Mr. Griffith. "Sensible, that is. Wrap up warm, then, and come along."

Arabel went into her mother's room to say she was going to Mortimer's Cross with Mr. Griffith. But Mrs. Jones was asleep and Arabel didn't like to wake her.

Then she called through the back door to Great-aunt Olwen, "I'm going to look for Mortimer, Aunt Olwen, with Mr. Griffith."

But Great-aunt Olwen's hearing aid was facing away from Arabel. She did not hear the message.

Arabel put her nightdress, and three ginger biscuits, which were Mortimer's particular favorites just then, into a little bag.

"All set?" said Mr. Griffith. "You best hop in the back with Sam. I don't hold with young 'uns in the front seat."

He let off his handbrake and rolled away, just as Mr. Jones came back with Chris Cross.

Arabel did not in the least mind going in the backseat with Sam. He was so large and warm that it was like leaning against a live haystack. His ears hung down on either side of her, and she fell fast asleep, curled up against him, and slept all the way to Mortimer's Cross.

When she woke, it was because Mr. Griffith was shaking her.

"Show a leg, dearie! Dead to the wide, you were. Here we are, and there's your Auntie Meg."

Auntie Meg, who was round faced and blue eyed and had black curly hair, seemed surprised but pleased to see Arabel.

"Ben never said anything about sending you, lovey," she said. "Company for me, you'll be, while Gwennie's in the hospital. Nice, that is!"

"I can't stay for long, Auntie Meg," Arabel said. "I just came because Mortimer got sent here by mistake, and I thought you might know where he was."

"Mortimer?"

"Our raven."

"Got sent to me?" Auntie Meg looked more and more puzzled. "Here," she said, "you'd best come inside, it's freezing and blowing like the Day of Judgment, and starting to snow, too. Come along in, Mr. Griffith, and take a drop of my elderberry wine."

Mr. Griffith said he didn't mind, and Arabel better watch out where she walked, the ground was like frozen spring onions. It was the middle of the night; Mr. Griffith had taken a very long time over the drive, because the weather was so nasty.

"Now," said Auntie Meg, when they were in front of a roaring fire, Mr. Griffith with the elderberry wine, Arabel with hot black currant juice, and Sam with a bone. "Now what's all this about Mortimer being sent here?"

"You remember that box, Auntie Meg, that you once brought us some apples in?"

After a bit of reminding, Auntie Meg said, oh yes, it was one of those Admiralty boxes, wasn't it. "We get a lot of them here, the lads from the radio station bring back the beer empties in them."

"Well, yesterday, by mistake, Great-aunt Olwen sent Mortimer to you in that box. Didn't you get a box with a raven in it, by motorbike messenger?"

"I got a box with the clothes in it that your ma sent. . . . No, wait a minute, there was another box, that's right," said Auntie Meg. "But it wasn't for me, it was addressed to the radio station; I told the boy to take it on up the hill."

"Oh, then that's where he'll be!" cried Arabel joyfully. "Oh, please, can I go up there now, Auntie Meg?"

"Well, now, hold on, dearie, it's a bit late to go knocking on people's doors and asking if they've got your raven. Suppose we wait till morning; then I'll give Commander Popjoy a call; heart of gold that man has; always one for a laugh; if your bird's up there, Billy Popjoy will soon have him tracked down for you."

"But it's snowing, Auntie Meg," said Arabel doubtfully. "Suppose Mortimer's out in the snow somewhere?"

"Bless us, child, he's got some sense, hasn't he? Find himself a place to shelter, he will, sure as you're born," said Auntie Meg stoutly. "Now, let's all get a bit more sleep, shall we?"

Mr. Griffith said he reckoned he'd bed down at Meg's for the rest of the night, if she'd no objection, as it was now snowing like a busted pillow, and he didn't fancy being frozen stiff as a haddock on the way to Bangor. So he went to sleep in Gwen's room.

Arabel, having slept such a lot in the car, woke up first next morning, and could hardly contain herself till the others were awake. As soon as it was light she began looking out the window, to see if she could see Mortimer anywhere.

She did not see Mortimer, but she did see the Admiralty Research Station.

The snowstorm had ended, and all the countryside was buried in a foot-deep layer of white, very thick and clean. At least that should make it easy to find Mortimer, Arabel thought, seeing he's so black.

Ice was everywhere, too, dangling in glittering points from trees and door handles and fences and telegraph wires.

The Admiralty Research Station consisted of a dozen low concrete huts, which were now up to their eaves in snow and looked like white pillows scattered about on the hilltop. Then, among them, there were three enormous radar scanners the size of huge circus rings tilted up sideways toward the sky. They were curved and white, like outsize soup plates, and they swung about majestically, this way and that, exactly the way that Great-aunt Olwen did when she was tilting her head, trying to catch what somebody said to her.

"Coo!" said Arabel to Sam the Saint Bernard, who was on the windowseat beside her. "I believe they're listening, Sam. I wonder what they are listening *to?*"

Sam didn't know, but Mr. Griffith, who had come to fetch Arabel to breakfast, told her that the great screens were listening to messages from around the other side of the world, and goodness knows where else.

"Supposing Martians was coming from outer space, or moon people, or flying saucers, those things would catch the sound of 'em far away, long before your ears or mine could."

"Coo," said Arabel again, and then she went to eat the hot porridge that Auntie Meg had made; it was much better than Aunt Olwen's with the black lumps in it.

After breakfast Auntie Meg was on the point of phoning Commander Popjoy when he arrived. He was a tall, bony, smiling man with a bright-pink face and a shock of yellow hair, and he wore shiny crackly leggings and a dark-blue waterproof, and hanging over that was a pair of binoculars on a leather strap.

"Wonderful weather for bird watching!!" he said. "Just on the way down I've seen a Snowy Boomerang, and a Jersey Cowfinch, two Arctic Snippets, and what I'm almost certain was a Great Western Night-Rail." Then he and Meg hugged one another, and he said, "Good morning, ducky," and she said, "Good morning, Billy, bach," it was plain that they were very fond of one another. Aunt Meg said, "Billy and I are going to be married as soon as Gwennie's out of hospital." Then she said, "My niece Arabel wants to speak to you, Billy, but first, what brings you down to the Red Dragon so early? It's not opening time!"

"Hoped I could use your phone," he said. "All our lines at the station are down; they're so iced over that the wires have snapped off. And I'm worried about the radio tower; the guy cables are iced over too: thousands of pounds of ice there must be, dangling on those cables. Lucky it's calm just now. Suppose a wind starts up, before the sun melts the ice. . . . If just *one* of those cables was to snap from the weight of ice, it might unbalance the tower."

"Dear to goodness!" Aunt Meg shivered. She glanced up the hill at the radio tower, an immensely tall steel mast; it stood among the radar scanners like a bamboo among mushrooms. "Would the tower hit this house if it fell?"

"No, but it might hit your old barn. Is there anything valuable in there?"

"Not a thing, but there was three hippie-looking fellows hanging around it yesterday at teatime. I told them to be off with themselves, they were a rascally-looking lot; I said that was where I kept the mad bull, but I don't know if they believed me."

"But what does your niece want to ask?" said Commander Popjoy kindly.

"Oh, please," said Arabel, "did my raven, Mortimer, get sent to your station yesterday by mistake? In a box that said Mortimer's Cross on it?"

"Well, we get dozens of boxes every day that say Mortimer's Cross on them," Commander Popjoy told her. "A lot did come yesterday, with valves and trivets and sprockets and gambrels in them. They haven't been unpacked yet. Would you know your box if you saw it?"

"Of course I would," Arabel was beginning, when Mr. Griffith had a bright idea.

"Have you anything on you that belongs to Mortimer?" he inquired. "Like, as it might be, a leg band, or a shed feather?"

Arabel did have a shed feather; several, in fact. She had picked them up from the kitchen floor after Great-aunt Olwen had finished bathing Mortimer.

She pulled some bent shiny black bits from her cardigan pocket.

"We'll give them to Sam to sniff and see if he can't run your bird to ground."

But Mr. Griffith's plan did not work. When Sam was given the feathers to sniff, his response was to give a gloomy howl, retreat to a far corner, and huddle there with his paws over his face.

"I'm afraid he seems to have taken a dislike to your bird," said Mr. Griffith, very disappointed.

"Never mind," said Commander Popjoy. "I've got a little bird scanner; my own invention, as a matter of fact," he added proudly. "We'll go up to the station and see what we can find."

"Can we go right away?" Arabel begged.

First, however, Commander Popjoy wanted to phone the big Admiralty station at Severn-side, to warn them that his tower was in a very dangerous state, and ask them to send over some hot-air generators to melt the ice off the steel guy ropes before the strain of the weight got too much, and one of the stays snapped, and the tower fell over. Luckily the Red Dragon phone was still working, and he was able to send his message. Then Aunt Meg thought she had better call Mr. Jones to say that Arabel had arrived safely at Mortimer's Cross. He sounded quite frantic with relief, when she did so, as he had spent the night phoning the police, hospitals, and the fire department to ask where his daughter had got to, and none of them had been a bit helpful. "Tell Arabel her Ma's much better," he shouted, "and Aunt Olwen's in the hospital, and I'll come and fetch Arabel as soon as I can." Then he lowered his voice and asked, "Is Mortimer there?"

"We don't know yet," said Aunt Meg.

"Well—" said Mr. Jones, "I do *hope* he's there, I'm sure, because Martha doesn't know he's lost yet, and she keeps asking for him; got a fancy to hear his voice, she says she has, don't ask me why, got an idea that it would help her to get better if she could only hear him grumbling 'Nevermore' in that way he does."

"Oh dear," said Meg. "Well, we'll see what we can do, Ben; we're just going to look for him now, as a matter of fact."

Then the whole party—Arabel, Mr. Griffith, and Aunt

Meg (who was free to leave the pub because it wasn't opening time yet)—piled into Commander Popjoy's Land-Rover, and he drove them, slithering from side to side, up the snowy track to the Radar Station. Sam stayed at the pub; since sniffing Mortimer's feathers he had been in a very gloomy frame of mind.

Aunt Meg had lent Arabel a pair of rubber boots that were much too big for her, but even so the snow came over the tops of them when she got out of the truck, so Commander Popjoy carried her into an enormous storage shed. Inside it were about a thousand boxes, all labeled MORTIMER'S CROSS H.A.R.R.I.S.

"Oh my goodness!" Arabel said in dismay, gazing around. "What a lot of boxes! Still, if Mortimer's here, maybe he'll hear us. . . ." She opened her mouth as wide as it would go, and called, "Mortimer! Are you in here?"

"Not *too* loud, ducky," warned Commander Popjoy. "We don't want to start a lot of vibrations. Let's see what my scanner will do."

He pulled out of his parka pocket a little black box, and opened it up. Inside was a little fan-shaped vane, made of gray pearly plastic, which began to twirl round and round when he pressed a button; and the box began to make a little quiet noise, *cheep-cheep-cheep-cheep-cheep.*

"Well now, fancy!" said Auntie Meg. "Isn't that clever, Billy, bach! Can it tell one kind of bird from another?"

"Well, it knows about size," said Commander Popjoy. "It makes a different noise for a thrush from what it would for a Whooping Swan. And it can spot any bird within a range of five hundred yards."

He began walking up and down beside all the ramparts, and stacks, and walls, and rows, and piles of boxes that said MORTIMER'S CROSS. He did this for quite a long time, and they all watched him. It was bitter cold, even inside the storage hangar.

Then Commander Popjoy's box began to go *twit-twit-twit-twit-twit*.

"It's picked something up," said the Commander. "We're getting warm."

He moved toward a box that was right up on top of a stack, with its flaps open. The *twit-twit-twit* grew louder. Commander Popjoy lifted down the box and looked inside.

"It's empty," he said, puzzled and disappointed. "But it seems to have an old blanket and some dried worms in it."

"Oh, then that *is* Mortimer's box," Arabel cried joyfully. "He must have gotten out of it and be walking around somewhere."

"*Twart, twart, wargle-wargle,*" said the Commander's bird scanner.

"It seems to get louder toward the door," said Billy Popjoy.

The whole party went outside again. Mr. Griffith carried Arabel through the snow. Now they were among the great radar screens, which looked as big as town halls when you were right beside them; and the tremendously tall radio mast, built of dark-gray steel struts, towered high, high over their heads. The steel guy ropes that tied it to the ground stretched away in all directions like the strands of a spiderweb. The ropes flashed with ice, which hung from them in a lacy glittering fringe.

"*Whatever* you do, don't touch those ropes," warned Commander Popjoy. Then he suddenly let out a yell of rage. "Who's pinched the lead off my radar scanners?"

"Lead, Billy, bach?" said Aunt Meg. "What lead?"

"There isn't any! It's all gone," he said furiously. "All

three of those screens ought to have lead backing. And someone's been and peeled it off them as if they were perishing oranges!"

"Pricey stuff, lead," said Mr. Griffith, shaking his head. "Fetch dear-knows-what an ounce in Bangor Market, it do. Maybe it was those three rascally chaps you saw, Miss Megan."

But Arabel bit her lip anxiously. Eating the lead backing off radar screens was just the kind of thing Mortimer might take it into his head to do; particularly if he were feeling upset.

Now, suddenly, the bird scanner's *wargle-wargle* changed to a *crawk-crawk-crawk-wheeeeeeee!* and, following its prompting, Commander Popjoy moved toward his radio tower and stood looking up.

They all looked up.

Arabel's heart almost froze inside her.

Mortimer the raven was about three quarters of the way up the mast, climbing steadily by beak and claw, hoisting himself up from strut to strut. He was so far up that he looked quite tiny, but there was no doubt that it was Mortimer; Arabel was certain of it the minute she saw him.

And the bird scanner was going *croop-croop-croop-croop-croop*.

"Merciful cats alive!" whispered Commander Popjoy, staring up through his binoculars. "A raven. *Corvus corax.* Or is it *rhipidurus*? No, I fear it is the common *corax*, but why, in the name of the purple pyramid, does it choose to climb up my radio mast?"

"Mortimer!" called Arabel gently. "We would rather you *didn't* climb Commander Popjoy's tower, if you don't mind. Could you come back down now, and climb it some other time?"

She did not dare call very loud. And Mortimer probably did not hear her. At any rate, he took no notice, but went on climbing, rather faster; he was very nearly at the top now.

Far away, at the bottom of the hill, some Admiralty hot-air machines could be seen arriving. They were bright-red generators, mounted on wheels; unfortunately they found it quite impossible to get up the icy, slippery hill. A lot of men jumped out of them and began desperately shoveling sand onto the road.

Now Mortimer was right at the top of the tower. He must have had a fine view from up there, Arabel thought; and apparently he thought so too. He hung rather nonchalantly sideways, and stared, turning his head around and around, like the scanners; stared at the white world stretching away for hundreds of miles in all directions.

"What does that tower *do*, Mr. Popjoy?" Arabel asked. "What is it for?"

"Why—why, it's used to send messages, ducky; it catches waves in the air, up there, and bounces them a bit farther."

"Could it send a message to Mars?"

"Very likely; if there was anybody on Mars to hear the message. Do you think your raven will fly down quite soon now?" said Commander Popjoy, his voice almost breaking with strain. "The way he's swinging about up there, I'm not sure if—"

"Mortimer!" called Arabel, a little louder. "We'd like you to come down now, please!"

Mortimer glanced down at her. Then he opened his beak. First of all a bubble of soap—the last—came floating up out of his throat; and after it had drifted away, with all the power of his raven lungs, Mortimer yelled "NEVERMORE!"—sounding as if he hoped and expected that his voice would carry all the way to Mars.

There was a short pause.

Then one of the steel cables snapped, with a musical

clang. The tower staggered slightly, like a person who has been hit with a banana peel. After that, in very quick succession, the other cables began to part and snap, as the tower jerked about, its weight being pulled first one way and then another by the tension of the cables that remained.

"*Down!* Get down on your faces!" yelled Commander

Popjoy. "If one of those cables hits you it'll cut you in half like Dutch cheese!"

He threw Arabel and Meg down in the snow and lay protecting them with his arms. Up above, they could hear the cables clanging away as if somebody were plucking a huge mandolin: *twing! twang! twong! twang! twing!*

Then there was another moment's silence; then a great shuddering wrenching grinding groaning *scrunch*, as if a giant's tooth had been pulled out, and the whole radio tower fell over on its side like a forest tree, neatly missing two of the concrete sheds, squashing a generator truck, and slicing Auntie Meg's barn in half like a pumpkin.

It took a long, long time to clear up the mess. Luckily nobody had been hurt. Arabel and Mr. Griffith didn't stay for the tidying up; they reckoned that they were more nuisance than help, and that it was best to get out of the way; specially as Mortimer, rather surprised by what had happened, came floating down out of the air to land on Arabel's shoulder.

"Oh, *Mortimer!*"she said. "Do you know what you've done?"

But Commander Popjoy, always a fair man, said, "Eh, well, don't blame the bird too much; after all, it wasn't his fault that the cables were iced over." So Arabel gave Mortimer a ginger biscuit, which he munched with a thoughtful air. And when, later, it was discovered that a gang of three lead thieves, known throughout North Wales as the Leadwaiters, had been trapped in Meg's barn by a tremendous tangle of steel struts, together with all the lead from the radar screens that they had been going to load onto a truck, the Commander was quite pleased and obliged to Mortimer.

Mr. Jones came up to Mortimer's Cross next day. By then it had started raining, and was much warmer, and the snow was melting splashily away.

"How's Great-aunt Olwen, Pa?" Arabel asked, after they had said a loving good-bye to Auntie Meg and were driving away from the Red Dragon, with some more apples, and Mortimer back in his own box, blanket and all; the Commander had kindly brought it down to the pub when he came to take the lead thieves into custody.

"Your great-aunt Olwen," said Mr. Jones, "is being driven back to Bangor by your cousin Stephen; she's going to stay with your aunt Lily till the plaster cast is off her leg."

Poor Aunt Lily, thought Arabel; but she said, "Who's looking after Ma, then?"

"Mrs. Cross from next door. She'll be there till we get home. And then I'll stay at home till Ma's better."

"That'll be nice," said Arabel. She leaned against Mr. Jones, sucking her finger, all the way home. "Don't you think you're too old to suck your finger?" said Mr. Jones. "Yes," said Arabel, and went on doing it.

When they got back to Rainwater Crescent, Mrs. Cross greeted them with a broad smile. "Martha's had an egg to her tea, and she's feeling quite perkyish."

Arabel went up to see her mother.

"Look, Ma! I went to visit Auntie Meg all by myself, with Mr. Griffith, and she gave me this blue sweater, made from Welsh sheep's wool. And we found Mortimer, and *he's* feeling better too."

"Was he lost, then? Where is he now?" said Mrs. Jones. "I've a fancy to hear his voice."

Arabel went to find Mortimer. He was looking at the buttons in her room. After a long, thoughtful stare, he ate quite a number of them. Then he hopped into Mrs. Jones's room and croaked at her quietly two or three times: *Kaaark*. "That's right, Mortimer, then," she said weakly.

Mortimer stood staring about the room as if he had forgotten something.

"What's the matter, Mortimer?" asked Mr. Jones in a hearty voice, coming into the room.

All the family were being rather extra polite to Mortimer, as if he were a visitor they didn't know very well.

Mortimer appeared to remember what it was he had forgotten. He went downstairs quite fast—flop, scramble, thump, hop—and dragged the umbrella stand across the front hall to the grandfather clock (the hands of which still stood at ten minutes to seven).

The door of the clock was open, because Mr. Jones had never been able to find the key after it fell out of his waistcoat pocket. Mortimer clambered speedily up and down the umbrella stand, fetching all his things— the dried worms, some of the buttons that had said I'M SORRY, MORTIMER, the cake-crumby blanket, the snail-shells, some ginger biscuits—and dropped them inside the clock. When they were all in, he clambered in himself and squeezed down on top of them. It was a tight squeeze, for Mortimer was, as Commander Popjoy had said, a fine large specimen of a raven. But at last he had crammed himself down to the bottom of the clock. There he sat on top of his treasures—which also included the clock key, twenty black cherries off Aunt Olwen's bonnet, and her spare hearing aid.

Arabel felt sure that he was wondering if his message had got to Mars.

MORTIMER'S PORTRAIT
ON GLASS

1

"Do you want to know about laser beams, Mortimer?" asked Arabel.

"Kaaark," said Mortimer.

So far as he was concerned, Arabel might as well have asked if he wanted to know about exports of methylated spirit from Westphalia. Mortimer was not interested in laser beams. All he wanted to do was to annoy the horse, Katie Daley, so much that she would break into a gallop. In pursuance of this aim, he was pelting Katie's fat brown back with cherrystones. Katie was taking no notice whatsoever; but after three or four of the stones had hit Mr. Jones, who was leading the horse, on the back of his head, he turned around and shouted: "Stop that, Mortimer, or I won't half give you a sorting!"

The Jones family were traveling through Ireland in a horse-drawn trailer, on their way to visit Great-aunt Rosie Ryan.

Where, you may ask, was Mr. Jones's taxi? It had developed clutch trouble as they reached a little town called Ballyshoe. A new clutch had been ordered, but it was going to take five days, since it had to be fetched from the other side of the country. And while this was being discussed, Arabel had noticed a whole row of horse-drawn trailers standing in the main square of Ballyshoe, waiting to be hired.

"Oh, *please*, Pa, can't we go on in one of those?" she begged, pulling at her father's sleeve. "I've *always* wanted to live in a trailer. And so has Mortimer, haven't you, Mortimer?"

"Kaaark," said Mortimer.

"And it would be much better than waiting here for a week while the taxi is fixed. We could go on and see Great-aunt Rosie and then come back here and pick up the taxi. Couldn't we, Ma?"

"That's ever such a sensible idea, really, Ben," said Mrs. Jones. "And it would be *ever* so romantic, traveling in one of them gypsyfied wagonettes: a real Romanesque holiday."

"Oh, very well, very well," grumbled Mr. Jones, when they had gone on at him for a while. "But it's against my better judgment, mind! Those things only go about two miles an hour. And who's going to look after the horse, may I ask? You don't just pour oil and petrol into a horse, you got to brush them and comb them and curry them and I don't know what-all."

"I daresay it's ever so easy, really," said Mrs. Jones. "They'll tell us about the curry at the hiring office; probably give you a big box of it there like those do-it-yourself curry kits they got in the windows of Indian grocers."

"*I'll* do the brushing," said Arabel eagerly. "I'd *like* to do it."

"Supposing its shoes need changing?" said Mr. Jones.

Arabel was surprised. "Mustn't horses get their feet wet?" she said.

"No, but sometimes they drop their shoes in the road."

"Oh well, Mortimer will keep a lookout for that, won't you, Mortimer?"

"Kaaark," said Mortimer.

So here the Joneses were, traveling at two miles an hour toward Great-aunt Rosie in Castlecoffee. (They had phoned her and said they might be a few days later than expected.)

At present their road lay across a huge brown bog which was called Black Feakle's Slough. As far as the eye could see there was nothing but flatness and brownness. Arabel had wanted to come this way because she had heard that there was a dinosaur's footprint on a small hill, right in the middle of the bog. She had always wanted to see a dinosaur's footprint. But now even Arabel was getting a little bored with the brown view; she was sitting on the steps of the trailer, as it rolled slowly along, reading aloud to Mortimer out of the *Children's Encyclopedia*. Mortimer wasn't listening. Mrs. Jones was taking a nap inside the trailer. And Mr. Jones was leading the horse, Katie Daley, along the road, because if he did not, she tended to come to a dead stop and begin eating the stringy clumps of heather by the roadside.

"I *knew* it would work out like this," muttered Mr. Jones from time to time. "Oh, my fallen arches!"

His daughter had offered to lead the horse, but Katie Daley was so large, and Arabel was so small, that she was not able to reach the reins.

"*Why* do you suppose a dinosaur stepped on the hill in the middle of Black Feakle's Slough, Pa?" she called.

"Wanted to get out of here fast, I daresay," grumbled

Mr. Jones. "And I don't blame him. This place is as flat as the perishing Siberian desert. *And* as cold."

It *was* cold. Arabel was wearing two sweaters. Mortimer had his feathers all puffed out. People they met along the road said it was the coldest summer since the French landed in Ireland, and that was over a hundred and ninety years ago. Icy winds were blowing down from the North Pole, and these were the cause of the unseasonable weather.

Katie Daley threw her head about so much and whinnied so loudly that Mr. Jones buckled her night-blanket around her. Arabel hugged Mortimer tightly, so that they could use each other's warmth, and went on teaching him about laser beams.

"Laser beams are made of light, Mortimer," she said. "Scientists have managed to squeeze a whole slab of light together into a thin stick like a knitting needle. And it is so sharp that it can cut through steel, or sew up people's eyes if they have holes in them."

"Nevermore!" said Mortimer, very amazed.

"If *we* had a laser beam we could stitch Katie Daley's shoes back on, Pa," Arabel said, "if they came off."

"Huh! I'd like to see a laser beam in this perishing wilderness," muttered Mr. Jones. "I wish we did have one. Maybe we could use it to fry up a few chips and onions. I'm sick to death of baked beans."

Just at that moment, Mortimer, whose sight was very keen, noticed something in the far distance, and let out a croak.

"What is it, Mortimer?" said Arabel. "Can you see a dinosaur?"

"Nevermore," said Mortimer. He began to struggle in Arabel's arms, and finally jumped down onto the road, and flapped off sideways across the blackish-brown spongy peat.

"Watch it, Mortimer!" called Mr. Jones. "You sink into the bog, no one's going to pull you out! And I mean that! I'm not risking my neck for no raven!"

However, the weather lately had been so cold and dry that the bog was not very boggy anymore; or at least not around the edges. It was like a bouncy brown mattress.

"Mortimer, please come back!" called Arabel anxiously.

But Mortimer went on walking across the bog. (He never flew if he could help it.) So Arabel jumped down from the trailer steps and went after him.

"Arabel, dearie! Just you come right back here!" called Mr. Jones.

But Arabel went on picking her way after Mortimer.

"I believe he has seen a dinosaur!" she called back to her father. "There's something kicking and splashing out there in the bog!"

Mr. Jones looped Katie Daley's reins around her front legs to discourage her from going on without him (which, however, she was not at all inclined to do) and began making his way gingerly after his daughter and raven, carrying the driving whip with him, just in case.

"*Arabel!*" he shouted crossly. "Where the blazes do you think you're going?"

"But look, Pa," Arabel shouted back, "there *is* something over there, a dinosaur or something, flapping about and carrying on."

"Well, I'm sure I hope it isn't one of those Bog People," said Mr. Jones. "You never know *what* you're going to come across in a back-of-beyond spot like this. I wish to goodness we'd never *come* this godforsaken way, that I do! Anyway it's as well I brought the whip along; I can always use the handle to punch whatever it is in the snout. Arabel! *Mortimer! Will* you come back out of there?"

"No, Pa, listen!" said Arabel. "I can hear somebody calling *help, help!*"

Now even Mr. Jones began to think he could see something. "I bet it's a black boggart," he muttered. "Or one of them perishing leprechauns they're always carrying on about. Leprechauns! I'd make 'em lep!"

But then *he* began to hear the voice calling *help, help!* "Bless my soul! If it isn't some silly bloke what's got stuck

in the bog! But what in the world did he go *out* there for? That's what I'd like to know? He must be a bit daft! Don't you go getting too close to him, now, Arabel, ducky. You can feel it's getting real unreliable under-foot."

Indeed, the spongy-brown mattress had turned to something more like half-cooked toffee, or chocolate fudge that has not set properly. Arabel was up to her knees in it.

"*I* think it's a man, Pa!" she shouted to Mr. Jones. "He must be right up to his waist in the bog. Why don't you throw him the end of your whip, and then we can pull him out by the handle?"

This seemed a good suggestion to Mr. Jones. The whip was a long leather thong, fastened to a thick, strong, wooden handle.

Standing on the firmest bit of ground he could find, a sort of lumpy tussock, Mr. Jones hurled the thong of his whip forward, like a fisherman casting a line.

But the bitter-cold wind was blowing so strongly from the other direction that it kept blowing the thong back to him again.

"Dang it! Plague take the perishing thing!" muttered Mr. Jones. "*Now* what's to do? *Arabel!* Will you come back out of that goo? You're up to your knees already. What your ma will say when she sees you, I do not know!"

"Glup! Gwilp!" shouted the man in the bog. He seemed to have mud in his mouth.

Suddenly Arabel had another good idea. "Mortimer!

Could you very kindly take the end of the whiplash in your beak and fly with it over to that person in the bog?"

She spoke as persuadingly as she knew how. Normally, Mortimer was the last bird in the world to do anybody a favor; he was not interested in other people's troubles. But fortunately, just now, he happened to be quite curious about the black, thrashing creature in the bog. So, after thinking about it for a long minute or two, he opened his beak, jammed the end of the whiplash in it, shut his beak again, and set off in a slow, reluctant, grumbling manner to fly the twelve feet or so across the bog. When he was directly over the stuck person, he began to hover on his wings like a hawk and dropped the end of the line.

"Oh, well *done*, Mortimer!" called Arabel, very pleased indeed, because she had not been at all sure that Mortimer would be inclined to help.

The muddy person grabbed the line, and Mr. Jones began to pull on the whip handle with all his strength. But for a while it seemed quite hopeless: like trying to drag up a cast-iron manhole cover with a spiderweb. Arabel went to help her father; she, too, seized hold of the whip handle and began to tug and strain. Nothing happened at all.

Mortimer, flying around and around above the person in the bog, now decided to take a hand; or rather, a claw.

Swooping down, he grabbed a clawful of something, snatched a beakful of the bogged person, all he could see sticking out of the mud, and then gave a mighty flap upward, shouting *"Nevermore!"* at the top of his voice. There was an equally loud yell from the person in the bog, and a tremendous explosion of mud, froth, and peaty water. Arabel and her father both sat down violently on the brown squashy ground as the line suddenly shot backward toward them.

"Don't let go! Keep on pulling, dearie!" shouted Mr. Jones, scrambling to his feet again, and he gave another powerful jerk on the whip handle.

Now the person on the other end of the line came right out of the bog, with a loud, sucking, squelching slop! and began crawling and sliding toward Arabel and Mr. Jones as they hauled on the line.

"Rare good whips they make in these parts, I'll give 'em that," grunted Mr. Jones, pulling away. "And just as well too, with all these-here perishing bogs about."

Mortimer, mad with excitement, was flapping around the person's head, making grabs at his hair and collar and ears; hindering, in fact, rather more than he helped. They heard a frantic shout: "Will ye be getting that godforsaken bird off me before he has the eyes out of my head entirely?"

"Mortimer!" panted Arabel. "I think you'd better come back to us."

Mortimer seemed quite unwilling to do so—he was really interested in the rescue operation by this time— but luckily, next minute, they had managed to drag the bogfast person onto a bit of ground that was firm enough for him to stand upright, and he did so.

Now they could see that it was a man, though he was covered with dark-brown treacly goo from head to foot.

"Kaaark!" said Mortimer, very disgusted indeed to find it was only a human they had rescued, and not a dinosaur. He was so annoyed that he shrugged his wings, let go of the man's ear (which he had been grasping in his beak), flopped heavily onto the ground, and began walking slowly and sulkily back to the trailer, kicking away bits of peaty soil with his rear toes at every step.

"Begorrah!" said the man they had rescued, wiping the black slime from his eyes. "Ye've saved me life, between ye, but I'm thinking it may have been at the cost of my ears! Yon carrion crow, or whatever he is, has notched them like postage stamps." And he rubbed them ruefully, adding: "Still, I'm not complaining. I'd have been a goner! I'm greatly obliged to the pair of ye!"

"What in the name of nonsense were you *doing* out

there on the bog?" inquired Mr. Jones rather indignantly, as they all began to pick their way with care back toward the road.

"Ah, well, ye see, I'm an entomologist in my spare time—that's a bug hunter to you, acushla," said the man to Arabel. "And I'd heard tell of a colony of the Large Pink Butterfly out on Feakle's Slough—very rare the Large Pink is now, almost extinct—so, seeing the bog's uncommonly dry this season, I thought I'd try my luck."

"And did you see any?" inquired Arabel, greatly interested.

"I'd a glimpse of some, alannah, I believe, but they were a great way off yet. 'Tis a shame I couldn't get closer to them before I began to sink."

Slowly and gingerly, the three of them drew nearer Katie Daley, the trailer, and Mrs. Jones.

2

Mrs. Jones had been enjoying a nap inside the trailer, but Mortimer's annoyed croaking and flapping on the roof above her had woken her up. When she looked out and saw the three black figures approaching out of the bog—for Mr. Jones and Arabel had also been fairly smothered in mud during the course of the rescue—Mrs. Jones let out such a screech that even Katie Daley

pricked up her ears and lifted her head from the scrubby bunch of roadside heather that she was chewing.

"Merciful cats alive! Murder! It's three Gypsy Mummies come out of the bog to cut our throats! Help, help! Ben! Arabel! Where are you? It's Black Feakle himself, risen from his watery tomb—or Black Treacle—and brought two of his fiendish lepidoptera along with him. Help, help! Ben, Arabel, where are you?"

"It's all right, Ma, it's us!" called Arabel reassuringly. "We pulled a man out of the bog. He's not a Gypsy Mummy—his name is Mr. Plunkett."

For on the walk back to the road the rescued man had told Mr. Jones that, when not chasing butterflies, he was a respectable factory owner, and lived not far off in the port town of Glasshaven.

When Mrs. Jones finally realized that it was her husband and child who were coming out of the bog with a stranger, looking like three mud-covered Guy Fawkeses, she was hardly less horrified.

"Oh, my poor palpitating heart! How do you *ever* expect to get all that washed off, tell me that, when there's only one little pink basin in the trailer no bigger than a salad bowl! I can't shut my eyes for *five minutes* but you're into some mischief, Arabel Jones, and your father's just as bad! I don't know, I'm sure it's enough to give a body the historical fantods just to *look* at you— I believe I feel one of my spasms coming on!"

"Ah, now, let ye be easy, ma'am," said Mr. Plunkett kindly. "Ye must all come back to Glasshaven with me and have a grand wash-up at my place—I've two bathrooms and all the hot water in the world. And my housekeeper will be after making a bundle of your muddy things and taking them round to the launderette. Sure, it's clean as mushrooms your husband and daughter will be in no time at all, missis, and I invite ye all to stay and have dinner in my house tonight, and I'll be showing ye round my factory."

This seemed like a friendly and hospitable plan, but Mr. Jones inquired cautiously, "How far will it be to Glasshaven, Mr. Plunkett?"

"Glory be, 'tis nothing of a distance! Twenty miles, if that. And my own car parked a step of the way along the road—I could be taking the lady in it if she wishes."

"Twenty miles?" said Mr. Jones. "Katie Daley won't do that in two days."

But, to his amazement, Mr. Plunkett unwound the reins from Katie's forefeet, snapped them briskly along her fat back, and shouted, "Musha, now, will ye!" in such a commanding voice that Katie instantly set off at a gallop, almost before Mr. Jones and Arabel had time to scramble on board the trailer.

Mortimer fell backward off the roof and was quite

cross because he had to flap his fastest in order to catch up again. However, once he was safely inside he began to enjoy the breakneck pace very much, and yelled with pleasure and excitement, jumping up and down a great many times on one of the well-sprung bunks.

"Yonder's the dinosaur's footprint!" called Mr. Plunkett, as they dashed past a little hill in the middle of the bog. On one of its sloping rocky sides could plainly be seen a set of marks like those made by six enormous toes.

"I wish I could see a dinosaur," Arabel sighed wistfully. "Look, Mortimer, here's a picture of one in the encyclopedia. It was eighty feet long and weighed fifty tons."

"Have one of those for Sunday dinner, you'd be eating shepherd's pie for weeks," said Mrs. Jones.

Now they came to Mr. Plunkett's car, parked by the side of the road where he'd left it to go in quest of Large Pink Butterflies. Mr. Jones was fairly sure that he would never be able to persuade Katie Daley to gallop, so he got into the car and drove it, while Mr. Plunkett continued to act as coachman for the trailer. In not much more than an hour they had crossed a row of grassy hills, and could see the sea ahead of them. Soon they reached a small harbor town.

"That's my factory," said Mr. Plunkett proudly, pointing to a long, gray stone building.

"What does it make?" asked Arabel. But Mr. Plunkett was not paying attention. He was staring out to sea and exclaiming: "Glory be to goodness, and isn't that an iceberg drifting toward the shore? Or am I not to be believing the evidence of me own two eyes? True 'tis the coldest summer since the French landed, but I never did see an iceberg so close to land at this season of the year!"

However it was quite evident that he *could* believe the evidence of his eyes and that it *was* an iceberg. It floated about a mile out to sea—a great green mountain of ice— and a whole lot of people from Glasshaven were crowded on the grassy cliffs and harborside, watching it with great admiration.

"Wurra! Yerrah! Musha!" they were all saying. "Did ye ever see the like?"

"Look, Mortimer, just look!" said Arabel.

"Nevermore!" said Mortimer wonderingly. He had never seen an iceberg in his life. Nor, for that matter, had Arabel.

However, it was too cold to stay on the dockside, all wet and muddy as they were. Mr. Plunkett took the Jones family to his house so that Arabel and her father

could get washed and change out of their muddy clothes.
There were two huge bathrooms, one blue, the other
green; even Mortimer was pleased to take a shower,
which shot out a sideways jet like the wake of a hydrofoil.
Meanwhile Katie Daley was turned loose in the paddock
with Mr. Plunkett's sorrel pony and a bag of oats; and
Mr. Plunkett, as soon as he, too, had put on clean clothes,
began to bustle about like mad, getting the garden boy
to take the Joneses' clothes to the launderette, and urg-
ing his housekeeper to cook a feast for the preservers
who had saved him from the bog.

"While it's cooking I'll show ye over my factory, and
we'll be taking another look at the iceberg, for it's a
grand sight entirely, and not one ye'd be likely to see
where ye live in London," he said. "Don't forget, now,
Mrs. O'Hegarty, the boxsty, the dillisk, the stelk, the
frumenty, and the carrageen moss!"

When Arabel and her father were dry and warm, and Mortimer had been persuaded to come out of the shower, and Mrs. Jones had put on some lipstick and a headscarf and her thickest jacket, they all walked back to the factory, which was on the harborside. By the water it seemed even colder; a freezing breeze blew toward them from the iceberg, which was drifting in with the tide, coming closer and closer to land.

Arabel (and Mortimer) would have preferred to stay on the wharf and watch the iceberg, but Mrs. Jones said, "Come along, dearie; it's perishing out here; and if Mr. Plunkett is so kind as to show us his factory, it's not polite to loiter outside."

"What does the factory make, Mr. Plunkett?" Arabel asked again.

But Mr. Plunkett and her father had walked on ahead, and she received no answer to her question. Mrs. Jones gave her hand a tug, to hurry her on, and, coming up with the two men in front, Arabel heard Mr. Plunkett say: "In the old days, of course, they used diamonds to cut the designs, but now we are more up-to-date and use laser beams."

"*Laser beams?*" said Arabel, very interested. "What do you use laser beams for, Mr. Plunkett?"

But Mr. Plunkett did not hear her. He was hurrying Mr. Jones inside the factory, eager to show him all his work. "That's right, that's right, come along with ye," he said, holding a big door open for Mr. Jones to follow, and Arabel, with Mortimer sitting on her shoulder.

By now it was well after teatime, and the sun was low

in the western sky, shining in sideways through the factory windows, which were very large and clear. As they came into the main workshop, Arabel gave a gasp, and so did Mrs. Jones, who quickly dived a hand into her pink raffia handbag, found her sunglasses, and clapped them on her nose. For there was such a flashing and a sparkling, such a shining dazzling spangling bright shimmering luminousness all about, that for several minutes, the visitors could see hardly anything whatsoever; all they could do was stand and blink.

"Kaaark!" whispered Mortimer.

"Well, blow me down!" said Mr. Jones

"Oh, Mortimer, isn't it *beautiful!*" said Arabel.

But just the same she was a little anxious. She held tightly on to Mortimer's leg, in case he should do anything rash. For Mr. Plunkett's factory was a glass factory.

There were cut-glass tumblers, and glass salad bowls, and great wide punch bowls, and tiny liqueur glasses, and great round brandy glasses like balloons; there were glass plates and glass clocks and shimmering rows of glass wind bells like organ pipes; there were rose bowls and wine glasses, there were cut-glass perfume flasks and powder bowls and delicately twisted long-stemmed flower holders, there were glass fingerbowls and pitchers and goblets and candlesticks. The light from the setting sun caught all the edges of the cut glass and threw millions of different-colored sparks all over everywhere, rose and green and tangerine, blue and purple and orange and lemon yellow. Arabel had purple freckles all over her face, Mortimer had a lemon-yellow

waistcoat. And the smooth glass all around them shimmered and shone and dazzled like a whole forest full of decorated Christmas trees!

Arabel thought she had never seen anything so gorgeous. She was still nervous about Mortimer, and held tight onto his leg, but she couldn't help being interested, as Mr. Plunkett began telling Mr. Jones how they cut the patterns on the cut glass with a laser beam.

"Where do you keep your laser beam, Mr. Plunkett?" she asked.

"Bless your heart, and isn't it a fair caution you are, and as interested and sensible as a grown person!" said Mr. Plunkett. "The laser beam lives here in this big box like a giant camera on a turntable, see, and we put a bit

of glassware in the jaws here, like this, see, and then switch on the beam—you can alter the power, for thick glass or thin glass, like this—and then you can write a pattern on a glass, easy as with a pencil on a piece of paper. Look now, acushla, I'll guide your hand and then you can write your name on the glass—this is the way of it."

So, with great care, and only a little wiggly, Arabel wrote

$$Arabel$$

on a tumbler, and Mortimer, breathing heavily, leaned over her shoulder and watched.

"Oh please, now can I draw a picture of Mortimer on another glass?" said Arabel. "He *would* like that."

"Arabel! It's rude to ask!" interrupted Mrs. Jones, but Mr. Plunkett said: "Sure, indeed, and ye can," and tucked another glass into the jaws of the machine. These were covered with velvet to prevent the glass from slipping out.

Arabel had drawn pictures of Mortimer so often that it was very easy for her to trace an outline of his big hairy beak, his feathery wings, his boot-button eyes, his long tail, his untidy trousers, and his sharp, horny claws.

"There!" she said. "There you are, Mortimer, on the glass!"

Mortimer looked over Arabel's shoulder and saw his portrait cut on the glass. And at that he was so amazed that, without even intending to, he did something that caused an absolutely tremendous amount of damage.

He drew a deep breath and yelled out: "NEVER-

MORE!" at the top of his terrifically loud, hoarse, croaking voice.

A high note played on a violin can shatter a drinking glass. And a blast blown on a trumpet can knock down a wall. And a peal of bells can break a mirror. And, in exactly the same way, Mortimer's shout of *Nevermore* shattered every single piece of glass in the workshop. Fragments and splinters fell about everywhere; sparks twinkled and shards tinkled; never was such a clinking and clanking, flashing and crashing, glittering and scrunching and scintillating and spangling and jangling, chiming, jingling, and twangling.

"Holy Moses!" said Mr. Plunkett.

And all his workmen were saying similar things:

"Bejabbers!"

"Glory be to goodness!"

"Mercy on us!"

"Begorrah!"

"Who'd ha' thought it?"

"Did you ever, in all your livelong days, see anything to equal that?"

"Sure and the bird must be the very divil himself!"

3

"Oh, Mortimer!" said Arabel. "*Look* what you've done!" Even Mortimer was quite startled and abashed. He gazed around him at the sparkling wreckage with his big blackberry eyes; he muttered to himself thoughtfully, and poked with his claw at a fragment of shining glass that happened to be lying nearby.

The only article in the whole place still remaining unbroken, as it happened, was the tumbler on which Arabel had drawn Mortimer's picture. That was still clasped in the velvet jaws of the laser machine.

Mrs. Jones gulped. Mr. Jones had turned quite pale.

"Oh dear," he began.

"Ah, now, don't ye be giving it a single thought," said Mr. Plunkett quickly. "Sure and the bird meant no harm. He doesn't know his own potentiality! 'Tis my own fault for fetching a raven into a glass factory; all the world knows ravens are unchancy birds. Bless ye, the insurance will be paying for it; do not yez be worrying your heads about this little mishap at all!"

Just the same, the horrified Jones family felt that the best thing they could do was to get out of the factory, and the town of Glasshaven, and be on their way.

"I'll—I'll leave you my London address, Mr. Plunkett," said Mr. Jones hoarsely, "and—when you've reckoned up the cost of the damage, you'll be so kind as to let me know the total—"

But at this moment everybody was distracted by one of the glassblowers. He came rushing into the workshop, calling out: "Will ye all be casting a look at the iceberg now! And it drifting clean into the harbor! And, be-

gorrah, it has a great beast inside it, like a starfish in a paperweight! Yerrah, 'tis the greatest sight this town has seen since the French landed!"

At this everybody (scrunching over the piles and drifts of broken glass on the floor) ran to the big factory windows to stare out over the paved wharfside and the oval harbor between its two arms of grassy cliff.

"Faith!" said Mr. Plunkett. "Did ye ever see the like?" And his workmen said, " 'Tis like a ship in a bottle. 'Tis like a chick in a glass egg! 'Tis like a walnut in a shell! 'Tis like a stone in a plum! What manner of creature might that be, at all, then? Sure, and its tail is longer than the racetrack at Fairyhouse, and its neck almost as long! How can the poor beast be carrying them two great appendages, now, answer me that? 'Tis no wonder at all it got frozen up in a hunk of ice, and best it stays there, I reckon. Do you suppose it is still living in there, the creature? Frozen alive, maybe, like a winter fish in a lough?"

Mr. Plunkett watched the landward progress of the iceberg with considerable anxiety: "Live or dead," he said, "if that chunk of ice isn't halted before it hits our dockside, there'll be little left of the port of Glasshaven, or this factory either! What yon bird achieved will be but a pennyworth of damage compared with this one!"

At these words of warning, everybody began to look very worried indeed. For although the iceberg was slipping along so smoothly, now that it was inside the harbor, everybody could see how very fast it was moving. It grazed, bumpingly, along the left-hand sea wall and

scrunched up half a dozen small boats like snail shells.

"Och, mercy on us, what'll we ever do at all?" somebody wailed. "If that hits the town, every soul in it'll be turned to meat paste!"

"Mortimer! I believe that's a dinosaur in there!" whispered Arabel. "See its long tail and its long neck! Oh, don't you wish that somebody would break the iceberg and let it out?"

"Nevermore," muttered Mortimer, a little doubtfully, and he cast a wistful glance at the laser machine, where the wonderful glass with his picture on it still nestled between the velvet jaws.

It was then that Arabel had her good idea.

"Mr. Plunkett!" she said timidly. "Don't you think that perhaps the laser machine could break the iceberg?"

"Glory be on high, 'tis pure genius that's in the child

entirely," roared Mr. Plunkett, and he dashed back to the laser box, spun it around until it was pointing toward the window, shouted, "Duck, everybody!" switched the volume up to full power, and directed the beam straight toward the approaching iceberg.

There was a moment of hush while everybody held their breath.

First the window melted and curled up like tissue paper on a hot fire.

Then, with a majestic, grating, squeaking, crunching rumpus, like the sound of a branch splitting off a tree (only a million times more so), the iceberg fell in half.

"Oh, the dinosaur!" cried Arabel in dismay.

For the dinosaur, freed from its container, had sunk stiffly into the deep water of the bay, and disappeared.

Now Mr. Plunkett was rapidly running his laser beam back and forth over the two halves of the iceberg, chopping them into smaller and smaller bits—rather like Mrs. Jones making bread crumbs before baking one of her apple crumbles.

"There! Thanks be to providence and the child's good thinking, now we can all rest easy," Mr. Plunkett said, turning down the power at last and switching off the laser beam. "Tom Foyle the harbormaster and his lads can be dealing with the rest of the ice that's bobbing around; they can be towing it out to sea with the lifeboat, or packing it away in sawdust for next summer's ice cream—if anybody in this town will ever have the heart to consume an ice cream again!"

Certainly it seemed improbable that anybody would feel like ice cream for a long, long time. The air in Glasshaven was so cold, from the closeness of the iceberg, that all the water had frozen in the pipes, and a small shower of rain had decided to turn to snow.

But nobody minded that.

"Well! Sure and we laid on a fine diversion for your first visit to Glasshaven!" Mr. Plunkett said to the Joneses. "Now you must be coming back to my house for a warming drop of something; and I'm sure by this time Mrs. O'Hegarty will be ready to dish up the boxsty and the dillisk and the stelk and the frumenty."

"Oh, but Mr. Plunkett—the dinosaur!" said Arabel urgently. "Don't you think somebody ought to fish the poor thing up out of the water?"

"Alannah, that dinosaur has been frozen inside that iceberg for more million years than you have fingers," Mr. Plunkett said. "And toes, too, likely. It won't hurt him at all to wait at the bottom of our fine clean harbor for a little. For the matter of that, it'd be a rare, strong line that was capable of fishing him up—'twould need more than a length of whiplash for that one! Let him wait. And now I'm sure you all want your dinner—as I do mine. Let you be coming this way now."

All the way up the wide, sloping, main street of Glasshaven, Arabel kept looking wistfully back at the waters of the harbor. And so she was the first to see the dinosaur heave itself out of the water and step over the cliff top. She thought it was like watching a horse climb out of a hand basin—there seemed so much dinosaur and so little water. The great legs stepped over the cliff as if it were no higher than a matchbox, and the wash caused by the great tail caused a kind of tidal slop along the harbor front.

"Oh, Mortimer," breathed Arabel for the second time that day, "isn't it beautiful!"

"Errrk," said Mortimer thoughtfully. Even he found the dinosaur rather large.

It was a greenish gray, very wrinkled, its hind legs were bigger than its forelegs, its teeth stuck outside its jaw, untidily, and its eyes were very small. Standing dripping on the cliff top, it did not seem quite certain what to do next.

"Dinosaurs have brains in their tails as well as in their heads," Arabel told Mortimer. "I wonder what happens if ever the two brains don't agree?"

It seemed as if some such failure in transmission might

be bothering this dinosaur—or perhaps it was just suf-
fering from the confusion of someone who has been
woken up too suddenly. It swung its head doubtfully,
on the long, long neck, gazed for a while at the town of
Glasshaven, lying below it like mustard-and-cress; paused;
and finally turned inland, striding away over the grassy
hills.

"Maybe we should be going after it, the creature?"
said Tom Foyle the harbormaster, a little dubiously.

"The folks at Derrycagher and Killinore may not be best pleased to have a dinosaur come leaping up the road, and they with no warning or expectation of the occurrence."

"We could give them a call on the telephone and mention that the beast is on its way?" suggested Will Byrne, Mr. Plunkett's foreman.

"Very likely there's no harm at all in the beast," said another man hopefully. "For don't I recall being taught in my schooldays that dinosaurs and suchlike did all be grass-eating animals?"

"No harm in it unless it steps on your house," pointed out Mr. Plunkett. "No: I am thinking we had best try to head it off. Maybe the Coast Guard helicopter could drop a lasso around its neck—or—or stun it with a rock."

"Some rock!"

"Maybe what's needed is some of those tranquilizing darts they have in zoos," suggested Mr. Jones, but not very confidently. "What the keepers use on tigers and gorillas, if they get fractious."

"Man, I doubt if there'd be enough darts in the whole of Ireland to deal with yon beast. If *he* gets fractious, heaven help us all!"

Meanwhile the whole population of Glasshaven ran up to the top of the hill, in order to see what the dinosaur would do next. And from that lookout point, everybody was relieved to see that it had not taken the road to Derrycagher and Killinore, but was walking straight in-

land. Every now and then it bent down the pin-sized head on the immensely long neck, and sniffed the ground.

"Acting like a bloodhound, 'tis," said Will Byrne.

"Poor thing," said Arabel suddenly. "I believe it's lonely."

And, as if in confirmation of that, the dinosaur suddenly threw up its head and let out a long, loud, wailing cry; such a sound as had not echoed over the world for millions of years. Then it went plodding on its way.

"The beast is heading for Black Feakle's Slough," said Tom Boyle. "Maybe somebody should warn it? 'Twould be a shame if the only dinosaur to visit these parts this century would go and walk into a bog, now? And that even before Danny O'Brien from the *Glasshaven Gazette* would be taking its photograph?"

But he spoke too late. For while the people of Glasshaven held their breaths upon the grassy hillside, their great visitor began striding over the distant brown flatness of Black Feakle's Slough. As he went on, he sank lower and lower into the soft and oozy ground. At last his head was the only part of him visible, plowing along like the periscope of a submarine.

Suddenly the head rose up—as if for a last look round— then sank from view entirely.

"Well, indeed now, and that's surely rid us of an awkward problem," said Mr. Plunkett, much relieved. "Come along home, now, let you, Mr. and Mrs. Jones and Arabel. Ye must be starving for your suppers."

So they went back to Mr. Plunkett's house and ate boxsty, dillisk, stelk, frumenty, and carrageen moss, all

of which were delicious. Mr. Jones was still worrying about the broken glass in the factory, but Mr. Plunkett said: "Ah, never give it a thought, dear man. If that darlin' child of yours hadn't had the grand notion of using the laser beam on the iceberg, there'd have been a deal more damage than that!"

"Errrk," said Mortimer sadly.

"What ails the bird?" inquired Mr. Plunkett. "Does he not like the frumenty?"

"I'm afraid he's thinking about that glass with his picture on it," Arabel said. "We left it in the factory."

"He can have it this very minute," said Mr. Plunkett. "I'll send the garden boy down for it directly."

And so Mortimer was able to go to bed in Mr. Plunkett's coal scuttle with the glass wrapped lovingly between his wings.

Next day the Jones family resumed their journey toward Great-aunt Rosie in Castlecoffee. But before that, they drove back with Mr. Plunkett in his car to see if there were any traces remaining of the dinosaur in Black Feakle's Slough. There was none—or only one. The bog had settled itself back into place—brown, flat, and gooey as before, like a huge plateful of molasses. But on the little rocky hill in the middle there were now *two* footprints. And a flock of Large Pink Butterflies could be seen fluttering above it.

"Maybe the dinosaur will come up again sometime, Mortimer," said Arabel. "Maybe he found a friend in there."

"Kaaark," said Mortimer. He was not really interested in the dinosaur. All he wanted was to sit gazing at the picture of himself on the glass.